"I'VE NEVER MET ANYONE LIKE YOU," ERIN SAID IN A shaky voice.

The admission sent a hot thrill through him. "What am I like, *chèr*?" Teague's words vibrated with need, dark and almost volatile in their intensity.

She stared at him, her face cast in deep shadow. The silence between them stretched out, the only sound the drums that echoed through the trees. Just when he thought she wouldn't answer, she spoke. "Dangerous. To me."

"Why? What do you think I'm going to do to you?"

She paused, then her trembling voice stroked him again. "It's not what I think you'll do, it's what I want you to do."

"What is that, Erin?" he asked hoarsely, taking another irreversible step forward in both word and deed. He lowered his mouth close to hers and whispered, "What do you want me to do to you, Erin? Tell me." He brushed his lips against hers. "Tell me."

"Teague." His name was no more than a gasp.

"That's right, *ange*. Say my name again." He touched his lips to hers. "Tell me. . . ."

WHAT ARE *LOVESWEPT* ROMANCES?

They are stories of true romance and touching emotion. We believe those two very important ingredients are constants in our highly sensual and very believable stories in the LOVE-SWEPT line. Our goal is to give you, the reader, stories of consistently high quality that may sometimes make you laugh, sometimes make you cry, but are always fresh and creative and contain many delightful surprises within their pages.

Most romance fans read an enormous number of books. Those they truly love, they keep. Others may be traded with friends and soon forgotten. We hope that each LOVESWEPT romance will be a treasure—a "keeper." We will always try to publish

LOVE STORIES YOU'LL NEVER FORGET
BY AUTHORS YOU'LL ALWAYS REMEMBER

The Editors

Loveswept ®801

BAYOU HEAT

DONNA KAUFFMAN

BANTAM BOOKS
NEW YORK · TORONTO · LONDON · SYDNEY · AUCKLAND

BAYOU HEAT

A Bantam Book / August 1996

ISBN 0-553-44537-5

Published simultaneously in the United States and Canada

Bantam Books are published by Bantam Books, a division of Bantam Dou-
bleday Dell Publishing Group, Inc. Its trademark, consisting of the words
"Bantam Books" and the portrayal of a rooster, is Registered in U.S.
Patent and Trademark Office and in other countries. Marca Registrada.
Bantam Books, 1540 Broadway, New York, New York 10036.

PRINTED IN THE UNITED STATES OF AMERICA

OPM   0 9 8 7 6 5 4 3 2 1

This book is dedicated
to the memory of my grandmother
Margaret Henderson.
From a covered wagon to a Chicago
bordello, you were New Orleans
born and the original moon-shiner.
I miss you, Gagaw.

ONE

It was a perfect night for voodoo.

Erin McClure smiled at the fanciful notion. Adventures were supposed to be fanciful. To her they had always been magical, like exploring a previously untold fairy tale. This particular fairy tale was her most private one. The magic that awaited her the sort that most only whispered about.

Zombis. Conjo. Hoodoo.

If they spoke of it at all.

If only Mac were still alive. She finally had the funding for their dream expedition, the one death had cruelly snatched away from her father. But not from her. She had no right to complain about anything. Mac certainly wouldn't have.

Yet, having spent most of her formative years romping in South American jungles, Asian swamps, African bush, and the Australian outback, she knew this trek into the wilds of southern Louisiana would be as sweaty and bug infested as it was exciting and magical.

She swatted at another mosquito as she climbed to the second-floor apartment she'd rented for the next three months. Actually, it was a refurbished loft in a mostly dilapidated row house. Still, it beat a lean-to or a tree house; she knew from personal experience.

A very unladylike bead of sweat dripped off the end of her nose as she bent to deposit her gear. She rubbed her face on the already wet sleeve of her Georgetown University T-shirt. Good thing she didn't have to be ladylike anymore, not in the classroom or attending endless college and business functions. Teaching in the former, begging for money at the latter. In the end, it had all been worth it. Every sip of tepid tea with the dean's wife, every soggy canapé eaten at another corporate we-have-money-to-burn-but-not-for-you dinner party, every glassy-eyed student dozing in the back of her botany class was worth it. Her dream had come true. She was jumping for joy.

On the inside.

On the outside, it was after two in the morning, she was over six hours late, and she had an eight-o'clock meeting with several professors at the local college who had agreed to work with her. Aside from providing a lab, computers, and access to their collected data, they would also be supplying her with a guide into the nearby backwaters and bayous. Without that important entrée into the notoriously closed voodoun society, her expedition could easily take two or three times longer than she'd planned. Longer than she had money to fund.

She dug in the back pocket of her gym shorts and extracted the apartment key that her contact at Southeastern University, Dr. Marshall Sullivan, had thoughtfully left with the landlord. Who had thoughtfully left it taped to his door. She smiled dryly. Bruneaux, Louisiana, was apparently not a hotbed of sin and crime.

It was just hot.

The moment she opened the door, she decided the sound of a humming window air-conditioner unit was the sweetest music she'd ever heard. It took less than three strides into the room to discover that said humming unit wasn't doing its job. The room was suffocating.

She groped for a light switch, flipped it. Nothing. "Figures." She let the moonlight guide her to the window, let out an uninhibited groan, and lowered her face to the blast of cold air chugging out of the air conditioner. Only after she'd fanned her underarms did she stop to wonder why the room was so hot.

A fluttering motion caught the corner of her eye. She turned toward what looked to be a small bathroom. "Aha."

The thin gauzy curtains framing the open French doors in the bathroom swayed gently in the night breeze. Bathrooms had showers. Cold showers. She eyed the soft invitation of the small wrought-iron day-bed positioned against the opposite wall. Cold water won. She cranked the window unit to high and paused long enough on her way to the bathroom to drag off her T-shirt and sports bra, then hop out of her baggy shorts.

She stepped into the bathroom, got to the open French doors, and froze.

Something was smeared all over the bathroom tile. Blood. Even in the dim light it looked like blood. A lot of blood.

It wasn't until she looked down and saw the dead man—the *naked* dead man—in the tub that she screamed.

Teague Comeaux flinched and made a half-hearted attempt to swat away the annoying sound. He wondered if the screeching banshee was heralding his welcome to hell. If so, then hell was really . . . well, hell.

He tried to open his eyes, managing only one narrow slit. Unless he was delusional as well as cursed to spend eternity roasting, that banshee looked a whole lot more like an angel. A naked angel.

He started to smile, then thought better of it. Ti Antoine had managed to get a pretty wicked left uppercut to his jaw. Teague's mind drifted from the disturbing replay of the night's activities—after all, if he were really dead, he didn't have to care anymore, did he?—back to his angel. His naked angel.

The screaming stopped. Naked Angel stepped cautiously closer. He tried to speak, but could manage only a low groan.

Bad move, Comeaux. He flinched, moaned again,

and let his eyes slide mercifully shut as she screamed once again. It was a short blast, but enough to make his head ring. Through the throbbing tattoo playing on his eardrums, he could have sworn he heard her whisper "zombies."

A second later hell went fluorescent.

Wincing, he closed his eyes tightly. He'd survived again. He doubted hell had megawatt lighting.

Just his luck.

"You're alive!" It was more accusation than relief. He could hardly blame her. Although most people got to know him first before wishing him dead.

"Who are you and what are you doing bleeding all over my bathroom?"

Well, he amended, maybe *angel* was too presumptuous.

After several seconds, he managed to crack open one eyelid. At least she was still naked. A small favor. As few and far between as they came, he made it a point not to pass on a single one.

At least in one area, they were starting off on equal footing. He was as naked as she.

"Hey, *mon tout nu ange*," he managed to get out with a voice that sounded as if he'd been drinking gravel instead of beer. "Join me?"

"You have about two seconds to explain yourself, *mon coquin voleur*," she said in a dead-on imitation of his Cajun accent. "If I believe you, *chèr*, I'll call an ambulance." She dropped the accent, her voice turned hard and flat. "If I don't, I call the police."

Under other circumstances, Teague would have

come up with a charm-them-out-of-their-pants smile and a toss-away line. Right now breathing, not to mention seeing straight, was enough of a challenge. Besides, she was already out of her pants. And he doubted his angel would fall for any line. Even his.

"*Coquin voleur?*" he repeated. "I may be big, *ange*, but I'm no thief." He watched as she took a bold step forward, stopping just short of being able to see over the high sides of the claw-foot tub.

"And I'm no angel," she shot back. "Time's up." She turned immediately for the door, offering him another favor he didn't pass up: the view of a sweetheart derriere.

And she was wrong about being in control.

"No police, *chèr*," he warned softly. The very last thing he needed was Frank Bodette, Boudry Parish's sorry excuse for a sheriff, stumbling around in his business. He was already doing a damn good job of screwing it up on his own.

"Too late." She had one hand on the door.

"Now see, *ange*, that's where you're wrong," he said quietly. "It's never too late." Not true. It had been too late for him years ago. But the lie rolled off his tongue with the ease of too much practice.

She turned back to him, still holding the glass doorknob. "You're naked, bleeding, and barely conscious. I hardly think you're in any condition to stop me."

Teague made the same tsking sound he'd heard all his life from his *grand-mère* Comeaux. And she thought he'd never learned anything from her. "Naked? Were you peeking, *chèr?* If I'd known, I might have thought that *coquin* comment was a reference to something other than my . . . height."

Color filled her cheeks and moved downward with the slow, sensual blush of heat. It surprised him. Other than the initial scream of surprise, she'd been facing down a bloody stranger, buck naked, with all the cool disdain of a debutante discovering one of the servants dipping into the caviar.

"*Coquin*, in this case, meaning the same as *voleur*. 'Thief,' 'crook.' Not 'big.'" She paused. "Though I imagine that derivation could be applied to your ego."

"Because if you had peeked," he went on, ignoring her, "you'd have noticed I'm not totally naked here." He winced even as his lips slid into a wide, unrepentant grin. "Unlike yourself."

She glanced down, obviously startled.

"*Tout nu, ange,*" he repeated helpfully. "Meaning stark naked. Angel."

It was then he realized her flush hadn't been a brief attack of feminine modesty. It had been anger. Even caught badly off guard by her state of undress, she barely let it show. Relaxing, meeting his eyes once again.

Intriguing, his angel was. He'd spent his first two beers earlier that evening wishing there was some way out of the predicament Marshall had unknowingly put him in. And the last two wondering what in the hell an ethnobotanist would look like. The one certainty he'd had was that whatever the answers, she meant trouble for him.

He realized now that he'd underestimated the situation on all scores.

She held out her arms and turned around—slowly—then placed her hands on her hips. Nice hips they were too. Flared out just enough to offset her waist. Balanced by breasts that weren't too small, or too big. Palm sized. Teague's fingers curled inward. She was tall, with shoulders of a swimmer, a flat belly and long, lean, muscular legs. Capable, strong. Graceful, but not soft. Nothing about her was soft. More Amazon than angel.

But she did have one hell of a halo. Her hair was short—very short—and sleek. Not golden, or something as mundane as blond. Her hair was pure undiluted light. *Cheveux d'ange*. Angel hair.

"Seen enough?" Without waiting for an answer, she snapped a white towel off the rack and wrapped it around her middle, negligently tucking it into her cleavage.

"Can't say as I've ever met a woman so comfortable in her own skin." For once, Teague spoke the unvarnished truth.

She lifted a barely noticeable eyebrow. "And I imagine you've seen a lot of female skin," she shot back, her tone hardly meant to flatter. She gave a small shrug. "Well, mine has been seen by hundreds of men, and, not counting that one little incident in Nairobi when I was eighteen, all of them have managed to control themselves. I suppose, with your experience, I should be flattered you're still conscious." With barely a breath she turned and said, "Now, I believe I was about to call

the police. I'm sure they'll appreciate your 'I'm not naked, I'm wearing a smile' line far more than I would."

Then she picked up his jeans. His wrist hit the rim
of the bathtub the same instant her hand found the back
pocket containing his wallet. Visions of gawking men
and erotic African adventures vanished instantly.

"Don't."

She didn't even look at him. "You're trespassing on
my property, why should I respect yours?"

"Because I'm not smiling anymore." Slowly, she
turned her head to look at him.

He released the safety and cocked the small black
SIG-Sauer 9 mm he'd balanced on the curled edge of
porcelain. "What I *am* wearing, *chèr*, is a gun."

Oh, wonderful. Erin quickly skimmed through several possible scenarios. Unfortunately, each one had the
same result. The bullet won.

Erin had learned early on that people rarely looked
past what you wanted them to see. If you seemed confident and in control, then, suddenly, you were.

But one look at the big Cajun overflowing her tub,
and she wondered if she'd finally met her match.

Arrogant, bloody, and for the time being undeniably
in control of the situation, she still had to admit the
man was beautiful.

She let her gaze drift over him as she continued to
think up and discard ways to regain the edge. One well-
sculpted calf rested on the rim of the tub, a flare of
muscled thigh barely visible. Then there was that rigid

vein running along his bicep. Which unfortunately led her back to the gun in his hand.

"Toss them to me, *ange*." The tone of command was unmistakable. He issued orders, people complied. Or else.

And that was her advantage. Because Erin was just as stubborn, just as determined. Maybe he'd met *his* match. It had taken more than three years of creature comforts to soften her.

She eyed the gun again, then slowly lifted the jeans. If she could get his pants tangled up with the gun, she had a diving chance for the French doors and freedom. She figured he'd probably assume she'd go for the bathroom door. It wasn't much, but it was all the chance she'd get.

"Don't even think about it."

Her gaze jerked upward. Had she looked to the open door? Given her thoughts away? She didn't think so.

And then it was too late. She'd made the mistake of looking directly into his eyes for the first time. All thoughts of escape routes and bullet trajectories blew away. There would be no escaping this man unless he wanted her gone.

His eyes held secrets. And magic. Black magic. She fought the shiver that began to lift the hair from her skin. He wouldn't miss even that small reaction. And while she could expose herself, her body, with bravado, she knew it would be foolish in the extreme to expose a weakness. He'd pounce on it. Use it. Use her.

She made herself study him again, working at appearing cool, unaffected by the threat he'd leveled at her. The least of which, she realized now, was the loaded gun.

His hair was a long tangle that fell to his shoulders. Shoulders he'd had to hunch forward to fit in the narrow confines of the tub. His eyebrows were dark slashes, neither too wide nor too narrow. His cheekbones were high and smoothly sculpted above a strong, even jaw that would have a five-o'clock shadow ten minutes after he shaved. There was blood matted on the side of his head, and the side of his mouth was swollen and discolored. But that didn't detract one iota from the impact of that mouth. He'd proven he knew how to use it, to tease, to command, to win. It was wide, generous, full, sensual.

"Toss them!"

She did, the reaction to the terse order purely reflexive.

He snagged them easily with his free hand. The gun never wavered. He nodded at the commode. "Now, close the lid and sit down. Hands in your lap."

She had to get out of there. Now. She had too much at stake. Fighting down panic, she struggled to come up with some workable solution they could both live with. *Live* being the operative word.

She started with a friendly smile, but it quickly faded when he shot one right back. Dear God, wasn't he beautiful enough? Well, in a wicked, dark sort of way. It was too much. He was too much. Filling the room, filling her mind. His control was too total, too absolute.

She knew she was making a big mistake. Possibly

fatal. But dammit! She had a once-in-a-lifetime appointment to keep in less than five hours. And she'd be damned if she'd let some bloody, lunatic Cajun with a gun louse it up without giving him one hell of a fight.

"Here's the deal," she said. "It's late. I have things to do tomorrow and you don't fit on my timetable."

He lifted a brow, his lazy amusement only serving to fuel her determination.

"Now, I appreciate you've had a rough night as well. And hey," she held out her arms in a gesture of friendly compliance, "I'm glad me and my tub could be of some help to you. I'm as much a Good Samaritan as the next guy. So, why don't I just get out of your way and let you get dressed, okay?" She smiled again, light, friendly, not a care in the world. "I hope you don't mind, but I really need to grab some shut-eye. Please, use the towels, the soap, whatever, and let yourself out the way you came in." She nodded toward the still-open French doors. "And close them behind you this time, okay?" she added. "It's hot as hell in here."

Without waiting for a response, she took a step back. She'd get either four hours of sleep—or an eternity of it. *Please*, she silently pleaded, *just let me out of this room.*

"You're amazing, *chèr*, you know that?" he said. "I imagine that 'I know best' take-charge voice works real well with those collegiate types."

Erin was so tense she half expected her bones to crack, but she slid another step toward the door. Something he said nagged at her, but she was too busy fighting for her freedom to worry over it.

She managed a tight little shrug. "Yes, well, one has to make do with what one has." Her mouth was dry as dust because all of her bodily moisture was running out of her pores. Another small step. "I imagine that lazy Cajun charm fools most people into thinking you're not the least bit dangerous either. Me, I appreciate that." She kept her gaze firmly on his eyes in a vain attempt to prove she wasn't scared of him. "In fact, if anyone asks, I never saw you. Never met you. Have no idea how that blood got all over my—"

He lifted the gun a mere fraction of an inch and with a short scream she turned and launched herself as far into the main room of the apartment as she could.

She hit the floor hard but ignored the numbing pain shooting from her elbow to her shoulder. She scrambled to her knees, only to get tangled up in discarded clothes and duffel straps. A loud thud then a string of curses echoed behind her.

She felt the floor vibrate under the weight of his footsteps. She felt more than heard him stumble as she frantically tried to claw the straps off her arms. *Don't shoot me, don't shoot me, don't shoot me.*

"Stop," he ordered from way too close behind her.

Sweat slicked her palms, making things worse. She swore under her breath.

"*Dieu*, would you just stop? I won't shoot you!"

"Yeah, right." Hopelessly trapped, she went limp in resignation. "How dare you do this to me!" she raged at him as she twisted around, putting her weight on her good elbow. "I know you couldn't possibly care, but

I've busted my ass to get to this point. You can't just waltz in here and ruin it all with one friggin bullet!"

She was breathing heavily, sweat streaming down her face, into her eyes. He was a blur, wedged in the bathroom doorway.

"I don't care who you are or what trouble you're in. I forget all about you, you forget all about me. Easy." She couldn't control the sudden trembling as exhaustion from too long a day took over. "I swear it."

He said nothing. She wiped her face on her shirt, then looked stubbornly back at him. And immediately wished she hadn't.

She swallowed hard. He was very large, very menacing, and very naked. Nothing about him was blurred now.

He held the gun loosely in his hand, his elbow propped on the doorframe. And, damn the man, he was smiling. She scowled.

"Now that is one thing I don't think I can ever do, *ange*."

"What? And don't call me angel."

He even winced beautifully. "Forget you. Easily or otherwise."

She swallowed again when his gaze dipped below her face. She groaned softly, knowing even before he pulled his other hand out from behind his back what he'd be holding.

"Drop something?" A white towel dangled from his fingertips. "I tripped over it." He eyed the tangle of clothes twisted around her and made that tsking sound again. "For both our sakes you really should learn to put things back where they belong."

Erin released it all—humiliation and indignation—in a pounding thump on the floor. "Go ahead, shoot me. I give up. You win. Happy?"

He wrapped the towel around his hips and moved slowly toward her.

"Aw, *chèr*, don't give up now." His voice sounded strained. "Things were just getting . . . interesting."

When he bent over, bracing his hands on his knees, her strength to fight came roaring back with a vengeance. She scooted rapidly backward, dragging the duffel and clothes with her, until her back hit the daybed. Clawing her way upright, she managed to sit on it. Obviously he was still affected by whatever wound he'd incurred. A momentary twinge of . . . what? Compassion? *For God's sake, Erin, the man threatened you at gunpoint!* She kept her attention split between him and the gun in his hand as she yanked the clothes from her sticky skin.

He started to waver and barely righted himself. "*Ange*," he said, roughly. "Come here."

"In your dreams," she muttered as she managed to shake out her shorts and jam her feet into them. Her shirt was inside out but she didn't stop to fix it. For all she knew he could be playing some sick game with her. Even if the only thing that looked really sick right now was him.

Don't even think it. Leave. Call the police. Better yet, go find the police in person and stay there until morning. Maybe they'll even let you take a cold shower.

"You can't go." The last word came out on a long groan.

"Watch me."

Just then he pitched forward onto his knees and fell to his side.

Good, she told herself. With a sigh of self-directed disgust, she looked back at him. How did someone so big and brawny, still clutching that damn gun, look so defenseless?

She caught herself before she took a step in his direction. "I'll call an ambulance," she said out loud, hoping, for some reason, that he heard her. "Anonymously," she added warily, confused by the conflicting emotions assailing her.

She grabbed her satchel, her hand was on the door—

"Erin."

She froze. Then, very slowly, she turned. One word, and he was once again in command of the situation. In command of her.

He was still on the floor, his back to her. The towel had slipped and she saw now the gash on his right hip. The discoloration and swelling on the back of his shoulder.

"Erin."

The shock of hearing her name a second time snapped her back to the moment. "How do you know me? Who are you?"

"Come . . . here."

She took half a step before she realized it and stopped. "How do you know me?"

"Dammit," he ground out. "Can't you . . . just once"—he groaned again—"do as I . . . ask?"

"You never *ask* for anything," she shot back. "And I can't think of one good reason why I should."

He rolled to his back. The towel had come loose and didn't travel with him. But her gaze was riveted to his face. He pinned her with those magic voodoo eyes and said the one thing guaranteed to make her do whatever he wanted.

"Because I'm Teague Comeaux. Your guide."

TWO

Stunned, Erin didn't move.

His head dropped back to the floor, his eyes closed.

"What the hell are you doing here now?" she demanded. "Like this? With a gun?"

No answer. Shutting the door none too gently, she stormed back into the room. He was out cold. Again.

She sighed, then looked longingly at the bed. "So much for sleep." She spared a thought for the phone. She doubted a man who clutched his gun like a teddy bear, even when unconscious, would appreciate men in blue or white right now.

Since he hadn't seemed too concerned about his injuries, she was willing to put the hospital off for the moment. And until she knew more about what was going on, the police were out too.

She stared grimly at her ticket into the bayou and voodoo country. He was half on his side, half on his back, all exposed. Every glorious inch. She pointedly turned her attention to his left hand. And still armed. That left one option. Letting him stay right where he was.

At least he was bleeding on the towel, she thought as she hunted down a lamp and flicked it on. Yellow light from the dim bulb bathed his body in a soft glow. What was she going to do with him? Several indecent and wholly female ideas sprang to mind, but she ignored them. He wasn't even her type.

She snorted under her breath. Who was she kidding? She was female and breathing. He was her type. Her only saving grace was the security of knowing *she* wasn't his. But then, as far as she'd been able to discover, she wasn't any man's type.

Of course, his requirements were probably not much more demanding than the female/breathing ones. Erin hated herself for the split second of yearning she experienced when she flashed on the two of them together . . . that way. But she was helpless to stop it.

The gun. She forcibly dragged her mind back to that annoying little detail. Erin debated the merits of easing the lethal thing from his grasp but dismissed the idea quickly.

With her luck she'd make him pull the trigger and wind up killing herself.

Instead she went into the bathroom, closed the French doors, ignoring the blood-smeared walls more easily than the shower nozzle and it's faded promise of cool relief. She dug up several worn rose-patterned towels, a half-empty bottle of grape flavored children's pain reliever, and a handful of plastic strip bandages.

She smiled a bit wickedly at the bright green turtles decorating the last item. Wouldn't he look cute in those. Well, beggars couldn't very well be choosers.

Stopping long enough to wet down a few washcloths, she crossed back to him. Staring alternately at the gun and his half-hidden face, she carefully nudged his thigh with her toe.

Nothing.

"Mr. Comeaux?" Still nothing. She crouched down beside him, his back to her, and dumped her small stash on one of the towels. She shook his arm. "Teague?" He didn't move so much as an eyelash. She noticed, half-distracted, that he had the thickest, blackest eyelashes she'd ever seen.

His breathing was deep and even. She prodded him a bit more firmly. Satisfied he wasn't pulling some sort of trick on her, she eased into a cross-legged position behind him and went to work gently cleaning out the shallow gash just above his hip. With a pair of nail clippers from her satchel, she fashioned a few crude, but effective, butterfly bandages from the plastic strips and applied them over the deepest part of the wound.

With a dry smile at the green turtles decorating his dark hide, she gave him a light pat on his perfect tush. "There you go, *mon Cajin ninja*." She pulled the towel over his hip and tucked it in—firmly—at his waist. "Okay," she said on a weary sigh as she scooted over a few feet. "Upward and onward."

It had been strangely easy to keep her eyes on his hip wound and off everything else. Anatomy, she'd told herself. Basic arrangement of bone and muscle. Despite the fact that he was just about as perfect a specimen as she'd ever encountered, it was still just arms, legs, hips, buns . . . perfectly sculpted buns.

Get a grip, McClure. Clearing her throat, she delicately probed the mat of blood-caked hair on his temple. Okay, so perhaps she wasn't as unaffected as she'd like to believe. As she needed to be. Even unconscious, he was a bit bigger than life.

Hell, she was only human, she told herself. But Erin had discovered long ago that her unusual life had stamped her with some sort of indelible mark that, even when she was playing staid collegiate professor, alternately bewildered and intimidated the men she occasionally dated.

Teague Comeaux didn't strike her as a man who'd ever been intimidated by anything life tossed at him. And picturing him bewildered was simply impossible.

Belatedly realizing she was stroking the side of his face, she tensed, inadvertently pressing on his wound a bit too hard.

He moaned, low and guttural. She yanked her hand away too late. Her neck had been taken hostage by a large, warm palm. One second later, he neatly flipped her over his back, her bottom tucked in the cradle of his hips, her legs still dangling over his waist. With her torso twisted against him, he dragged her face to his.

Glassy black eyes bored into hers. He wasn't choking her, but there was no mistaking the strength in his fingers. She didn't try to move.

"What the hell are you doing?" he asked, his voice not more than a rasp, his eyes still clouded with pain.

She swallowed slowly. "Playing Nurse Ratched?"

He winced sharply when his smile tugged at the split skin on of his lip. "*Mais yeah*, Florence Nightingale you're not, *ange.*"

"No point in pretending to be something you're not."

The smile disappeared from his eyes instantly, and Erin felt the hair on her arms and neck rise. She swallowed again, but this time she tasted a tiny bit of fear.

"I'd appreciate having my neck back, thanks," she said with all the bravado she could muster.

He loosened his hold but kept his fingers pressed to the skin covering her pulse. Her rapid pulse. So much for cool. Erin wondered if she'd ever have any secrets from this man. Even the tiny, sanity-saving ones.

No. Teague Comeaux wouldn't let her have even the smallest edge. Ever.

"Why didn't you leave?" he asked quietly.

Good question. "You know damn well why."

"Smart girl."

She veered sharply from feeling like a small trapped animal to feeling supremely human and very female. The only similarity between the two was the fear of being devoured. Whole.

Trying to forget she was draped across his mostly naked body, Erin discovered that looking into his eyes was just as fraught with danger. But maintaining eye contact was a universal method of proving strength, equality, invincibility. And the only prayer she had of getting off this floor.

"Why didn't you just tell me right off who you were?"

"I was a bit out of it, *chèr*," he reminded her. "Until your lovely screech woke me up." He seemed amused by her scowl. "And then there was that show you put on. What man in his right mind would stop that?"

"We'll never know, will we?"

The deep grumble of sound he made might have been a chuckle, she wasn't sure. She was too busy feeling his body move under hers. "Since you know I won't run, can we get off the floor?"

His finger traced a lazy pattern along the vein in her neck. "The floor's not so bad, *ange.*"

Erin's blood warmed and seemed to pool low in her belly. "Let me up," she said roughly, not caring what he saw, what he knew he was making her feel.

He released her neck, but when she moved to slide off, he held her captive again with one finger to her chin. "This time."

Careful not to hit his wounded hip, she lifted herself off him and scooted several feet away before standing and moving to a small, overstuffed chair.

Facing him now, she sat down and braced her elbows on her knees. "Let's get one thing straight up front. I'm here to do research on a project I've dedicated most of my life to. Not to indulge in some steamy bayou affair with the local parish stud."

"And here I thought my reputation had spread statewide."

His tone told her he wasn't the least bit intimidated by her words. But he didn't bother to deny the proposition he'd clearly made. Hell, he was a living, breathing proposition just lying there doing nothing.

She barged ahead. "I appreciate your taking me into the bayou. I know you realize how important your role is in my research. And because of that I'm willing to overlook being held at gunpoint and having my room invaded."

"No questions?" Gone was the teasing scoundrel. He looked wary. The predator, sniffing the air for danger once again.

She squared her shoulders. "Just one."

"Shoot."

She glanced at the gun. "Very funny."

"I aim to amuse, *chèr.*"

I'll bet you do. "I'm counting on you to get me in, to be a sort of translator/guide/ambassador." She sighed heavily when he quirked his brow at the last part. "You know these people, right? So they're used to you." Her tone clearly said she couldn't fathom such a thing. "Are you prepared to do this?"

"I'll do my best."

"Okay then, we have a deal."

"That's it? No more questions about tonight? About this?" He lifted the gun off the floor.

"Would you answer them honestly?"

"Probably not."

"Then why bother, right?" Pressing her palms against her knees, she stood. "You're not expecting anyone else to crash in here tonight, are you?"

"At this late hour?" The rogue smile returned. "Why that would be so rude, *mon chèr.*"

"Yes, I'm sure your friends, that's accepting you have any, are all well-mannered gentlemen."

"We may not be the classiest bunch, but we know how to treat people right, *ange.*"

"Yeah." She gestured to his bruised forehead and swollen mouth. "I can see that."

"Aw, *chèr*, that weren't nothing but a little barroom brawl between longtime acquaintances."

"A real fun date, I'm sure," she said dryly. "All this and live ammo too."

He chuckled, then winced and held his hand to his mouth. "And here I didn't plan on liking you very much."

She arched one brow. "Yeah, us ethnobotanists are always getting a bad rap."

"I can see that."

The quietly spoken words unnerved Erin as nothing else had so far. "Can you point that thing somewhere else?" she snapped.

Teague looked down at himself, then up at her. "You want to clarify that, *ange?*"

"The gun," she ground out. "The deal, remember?" Gun or not, she turned her back to him and poked into her duffel. Dragging out a pair of baggy, ratty sweats, she tossed them at him. "Here, I imagine they'll be a bit short, but probably easier to get into than your jeans." She nodded to the small pile next to him. "There's some alcohol and wet washrags and children's medicine. That's the best I could do. Help yourself. I've got to get some sleep. I have an appointment in—" she looked at her watch and groaned, "four hours."

Without further hesitation, she stalked to the small wrought-iron bed and drew off the chenille spread.

"Does this mean I don't get the bed?"

She climbed under the sheet and turned her back to him. "I believe the tub is still available."

"You're more than kind, *chèr*."

She rolled to her back and glared at him. "Considering you could be sitting in jail right now, you'd better believe it. But be warned, I'm still mad about not getting my cold shower. You owe me for that one."

"Anytime, *ange*." The words were too soft, too throaty. "Anytime."

Teague watched her thump her pillow and rustle under the covers a moment or two, then she was still. He spent another few minutes watching her breath move evenly in and out. She fell asleep even more easily than he did. Which, considering where he'd ended up tonight, really said something.

And just how the hell had he ended up naked in her tub? With a silent groan, he pushed to a sitting position, then gingerly probed the side of his head. Ti Antoine. The sneaky bastard. That answered how he'd ended up bloody. The rest was still a bit blurry.

One thing was certain. The stupid fight he'd been suckered into had cost him a very important meeting. Ti Antoine—all three hundred and twenty-five pounds of him—was a drunk and a bully, and he didn't have to be the former to be the latter. But he'd been plenty drunk that night.

Teague was well aware that Ruby had probably egged him on, taunting him with what Ti wanted and sure as hell would never get. But nobody messed with Teague's waitresses. Not that Ruby would thank him for his intervention. She preferred to fight her own battles. God knows she'd wielded that heavy serving platter like an Amazon warrior.

His fingers hit a sore spot and he flinched, then swore under his breath as he mentally tallied how much two new barstools, three tables, five pool cues, and half a dozen beer mugs would cost him. Hell, he owned the damn bar. He'd just add it to Ti's bar bill. He drank so much he'd never know anyway.

He just hoped Skeeter could set up another drop point. If he missed the next shipment, he'd be stuck down here for at least another six months, setting up another sting. If he didn't get himself killed first.

And lately that had been looking like the better alternative. Hell, who was he kidding? If it wasn't for Grand-mère and what he owed her, he'd have stepped in front of a bullet years ago.

He sighed in frustrated defeat. It had always been family. Twisting him around and binding him up, when all he'd ever wanted was to be free of them all forever. Something he'd long ago realized would never happen. Family didn't go away. It was a life sentence, no matter how you looked at it.

Like now. After almost a year, it looked as if he was finally going to pull off the bust, keep Grand-mère clear of the hassle, and once and for all get the hell out of Louisiana. Nothing and no one could draw him back this time. This would make them square. Even up whatever debt he thought he had. They'd always be tied to him, but he sure as hell didn't have to live with them.

And now, bingo! Out of the blue, Marshall—who had made a point of never asking Teague for a damn thing—comes out of nowhere with his baby-sitting request. The last thing Teague needed was some flower-hunting scientist stomping all over the bayou . . . and his operation. But Marsh had made it clear she'd stomp with or without a guide and, having met her, Teague didn't doubt his half-brother's assessment.

Teague slowly rolled to his knees and stood, snagging the sweatpants at the last second but leaving the towel where it fell. He stayed bent over for some time, certain not to make the same mistake he had earlier. Passing out again at this point was unacceptable.

He'd already let the evening's events get way too out of hand.

When he was certain he wouldn't get light-headed, he rolled his spine up straight, lifting his head last. His vision was blurry and his body felt as if it had been used for . . . well, exactly what it had been. Target practice with a barstool.

He made his way slowly back to the bathroom. Christ Almighty, had all that blood come from him? Damn head wounds bled like a stuck pig. He spied his once white T-shirt wadded up in the corner behind the claw-foot tub, where it had apparently landed. That explained the blood smears on the wall. He dimly recalled yanking it off, along with his jeans, and climbing into the tub with the intent of cleaning up.

Hell, at least he'd tried to make himself presentable. Dr. McClure should be impressed.

Dr. McClure. Teague stood in front of the partially silvered mirror and stopped fighting the urge to think about her in more detail. He told himself it helped divert the pain of examining the gash on his temple, but it wasn't flashes of her strong, lean, naked body that invaded his mind. She was put together nice enough, but Teague had seen his share of naked women.

It was her bravado and frank honesty that had captured his attention. *Vigueur*, his *grand-mère* would call it. Strength, force.

Marshall hadn't really said much about her and Teague hadn't wanted to know. He'd been so surprised that his half-brother had asked him for help that he hadn't taken time to question him too deeply. When he'd thought of it at all—beyond the pain-in-the-ass aspect of it—he'd pictured some dried-up, earth-hugging, bookworm type whose passions ran to spouting Latin plant names. He thought of the woman lying semicomatose in the next room.

Oh, Erin was passionate all right. Teague smiled, reopening the cut on his lip, not caring. An imposition and pain in the ass for sure, but she also intrigued him. Too much.

And he was going to do absolutely nothing about it.

Eyeing the tub behind him, Teague carefully moved over and twisted the cracked ivory handles. If he was going to sleep in it, he'd use some cool water for a mattress. He wet a towel and made a half-hearted attempt at cleaning the walls, stopping when he realized he was just making it worse.

He needed rest, needed to be alert and on the ball. He'd clean up the mess in the morning.

A long, low groan escaped his lips as he cautiously lowered himself into the tepid water.

Something tugged at his hip. He reached back and pulled it off, examining the plastic bandages as he leaned his head back against the rim and slipped lower into the water.

"What in the hell?" He frowned as he made out the small cartoon characters wielding swords and shields. His gaze drifted to the open bathroom door and the sheet-draped mound huddled in the small bed. *Who are you, Erin McClure?*

He let his eyes slide shut. One hand dangled over the back of the tub, the gun lying within easy reach on a footstool, hidden from view.

He curled the fingers of his other hand around the crumpled bandages and drifted off to sleep.

THREE

"We simply have to stop meeting like this."

Teague didn't bother to open his eyes. He wasn't sure why. He just knew he shouldn't start the day being charmed by her.

"Sounded like a herd of buffalo routing around in there, *ange*," he said lazily. "You always such a considerate hostess?"

"To be a hostess, there has to be an invited guest." She stalked into the room without so much as a glance in his direction—he knew, he peeked—and closed the French doors he vaguely remembered opening after he'd drained the tub at some point during the night. Place had been a damn refrigerator.

"I have to be downtown in an hour," she went on, all business. "I'm hot. I want a shower." A stifled sigh.

Probably looking at the blood smears, he thought. They'd look a lot worse in daylight. Another reason to keep his eyes shut.

"I *need* a shower."

"Sounds like you need a strong cup of chicory, *chèr*. Are you always like this in the morning?" Startling images of a variety of things he could do to put a smile on her face made him shift a bit. He was even more certain he shouldn't start off fantasizing about taking her to bed for the rest of the day.

"Clean up your mess and be out of here in five minutes."

Teague cracked open one eye. "Or else?" He didn't bother picking up the gun again.

She planted her hands on her hips. "I've been trained in jungle warfare our military has never even dreamed of. Use your imagination." With that, she stalked back into the other room.

Helpless against it, Teague smiled.

Erin was smoothing the wrinkles from a pair of poorly packed khaki pants when she felt him behind her. Clear across the room in the doorway, but she could feel him nonetheless. It was like the damn man had a palpable aura of heat hovering around him. Probably due to all the pheromones women sent shooting his way, she thought irritably.

She'd spent a good part of what little rest she'd gotten the night before tossing and turning. But then a naked, bloody Cajun sleeping in one's bathtub didn't exactly make for sweet dreams.

Liar.

She quickly pulled a soft print blouse from her duffel bag and shook it out with an audible snap.

"All yours, *ange*."

That's just what I'm afraid of, she thought darkly.

She straightened and turned to him. She froze for a heartbeat as she looked at him for the first time that morning. Bright sun was already streaming through the doors at his back, reflecting off his smooth skin, casting his muscles in stark relief. Freshly showered, with his black hair combed back from his stunning face, he made her breath catch in her throat. Even black and blue, the man had an almost overwhelming presence. The white towel tucked firmly around his waist accentuated just how dark he was. Dark skin, dark hair, dark eyes.

"Thought you were in a hurry, *chèr.*"

That mouth . . .

She jerked her gaze up to his eyes. "I am."

He moved from the doorway. She swallowed hard. Gone was the weaving, beaten man of the night before. He took only a couple of steps, but the natural grace and control he had over his large frame was crystal clear. She didn't miss the fact that the gun was nowhere in sight. Just as she didn't miss the fact that this morning, he didn't need it.

He stopped several feet away, water drops still glistening on the small patch of black hair swirling between his pectorals.

"Then stop staring at me as if you have all the time in the world and you're just looking for someone to waste a couple of hours of it with." He took another step. "I have things to do today, too, *chèr.* But that's the sort of invitation no man in his right mind would turn down."

Erin lifted her gaze from his chest to his eyes, suddenly finding the ironic humor in the situation. "Well, I guess I've been mingling with lunatics then."

His smile showed his surprise. "I guess you have."

Realizing her plan was backfiring badly, she cleared her throat and turned back to her clothes, not caring if he read cowardly retreat into her actions.

She was the type of woman who attracted the pocket protector set. When she attracted anyone at all. She wasn't even sure if Teague Comeaux owned a shirt, much less one with a pocket.

"Yeah, well, whatever the case may be, I don't have time to waste. I'll have Marshall contact you when I'm ready to make contact with the *bokor*."

He moved so fast she didn't hear him. His hand closed around her arm, bringing her sharply around to face him.

"*Bokor, mon chèr?*" His voice was flat, deadly cold, his eyes glittering black . . . and empty.

The total lack of emotion made Erin shiver.

"For a supposed expert, you haven't done your research too well, *ange*."

She yanked her arm. He released it, raising his hand palm out before dropping it to his side, as if touching her hadn't been his choice.

She flexed her arm once, resisting the urge to rub it. He hadn't held her tightly, but the sensation of his fingers pressed into her skin wasn't fading. Not that she'd wanted to be touched by him either.

She looked him in the eye. "My research is thorough and my sources impeccable. Are you telling me you don't have a connection with the *bokor?* Because if you don't, you're wasting my time."

"A *bokor* serves with the left hand. Uses the black magic," he clarified. "Belisaire follows the *Rada*, the positive. She understands the *Petro*, the dark side, but only as a means to combat it. You don't want to mess with that, *chèr.* No one does."

"Don't condescend to me. I have researched voodoo and it's various counterparts in Haiti, Africa, the islands. I'm well aware of the dangers involved in my project."

Teague closed the space between them with one step, but didn't touch her. He didn't have to.

"You have no idea what you're getting into, *chèr.* You go into the swamps alone, here . . . you may not come out."

Erin's skin burned at the heat rolling off him. The heat in his voice, the heat in his eyes, the heat of his near naked body so close to hers.

"I know what I have to do," she said, hating that her voice was barely more than a whisper.

Teague leaned closer. She felt his breath fan across her cheeks, brush over her lips. "So do I, *ange.* So do I." It was the unexpected note of resignation in his voice that kept her from moving away as he dropped his head, angling his mouth toward hers.

Dear God, he was going to kiss her. Erin's thighs tightened together without her consent. He lifted his hand and cupped her face, lifting her mouth to his.

His palm was a hot brand on her cheek and she jerked away, taking several steps back. *What the hell was she doing?*

Her entire body was screaming in sudden frustration. "I—I have to get a shower. I have to go."

That Teague looked almost as disconcerted as she felt did little to calm her. She'd expected some cocky, arrogant retort, mocking her obvious inexperience. She realized she was going to have to stop expecting him to do the expected. She also realized she was going to have to get the hell out of here while the getting was good.

Snatching up her clothes, she stepped around him, very aware he didn't so much as move an inch. She turned at the bathroom door, facing him. "Can you or can you not introduce me to the local voodoo priest, your *houngan?*"

"Priestess."

"The *mambo*, then. Can you?"

"I can."

Not entirely satisfied with his easy answer, she asked, "Will you take me to her?"

"Yes."

Erin released a breath. "When?"

Teague visibly relaxed, that crooked smile once again curving his wide lips. "You don't exactly make an appointment with Belisaire. I'll find you when the time is right."

Erin opened her mouth to argue that she needed something more definite, but shut it again. Marshall had been vague about many things, but he had made it clear that Teague wasn't just her best connection, he was her only one.

"Fine. You can reach me here or on camp—"

"I know how to find you."

Erin shivered at the promise in his words. She simply nodded, then shut herself in the bathroom, locking the door behind her. As if that would stop him.

If Teague Comeaux wanted something, she doubted anything would stop him.

She peeled off her clothes, gasping softly as the fabric rubbed against her erect nipples. The image of a man like Teague, all dark and dangerous, wanting her, taking her . . .

Her thighs tightened against the renewed ache between her legs.

She was a scientist. A woman who saw life as something to be examined, understood, related to fact. Her body was a complex, fascinating machine, one she knew inside and out and was completely comfortable with.

On a scientific level.

She glanced up into the mirror. Her cheeks were flushed. Her eyes bright. She suddenly felt out of control. A stranger to her body's responses.

The idea of being wanted like that was a seductive thrill she'd never felt. That she liked it was even more frightening. Was it so bad to want to be wanted like that? To want to be taken by a man like him? Just once?

Erin's fingers curled, digging into her palms, fighting against the sudden need to do something, anything, to ease her body's torment.

And if she did, would once be enough?

Teague slammed the phone down. "Damn, damn, damn." Skeeter had taken off for parts unknown when

Teague blew their meeting. He'd spent a day and half trying to track his partner down. No luck. Ten months of hard work possibly down the drain.

There was a light tap on the half-open door to the small cluttered office he kept at the back of the Eight Ball, the pool hall and bar he owned as a cover.

"What?" he barked.

A blond head poked in the door. "Hey, you busy?" Marshall stepped into the room.

"What brings you down to the swamps?" Teague asked, honestly surprised. His brother had visited Teague here precisely once in the year he'd been back. Then it had been to ask him for the one and only favor Marsh had ever requested. Teague didn't doubt a certain ethnobotanist was his reason for this visit as well.

"Well, I'm not here for a game of eight ball."

The one thing that Teague appreciated about his half brother was that, unlike most of their family, Marshall didn't play games. You always knew where you stood with him.

"Good thing. Those boys out there would take half your trust fund before you downed your first beer."

Marshall didn't take the bait. But then, he never did. And if he noticed Teague's battered face, he didn't mention it. Not for the first time, Teague wondered what Marsh really thought of him. Did he have any idea what kind of man Teague had become? Did he care?

And why did any of it matter now?

Marsh brushed off a folding metal chair and sat. His Italian leather loafers, hand-tailored pleated trousers, rumpled white linen shirt, loose designer tie, wire-rim glasses, and disheveled blond hair made him look like exactly what he was: a slightly harried professor who happened to be swimming in family money.

"Yeah well, they can have it."

Teague smiled, on familiar ground now. "Father on your case to leave the ivy-covered walls of the university for the ivy-covered walls of the Sullivan law practice again?"

Marshall ignored the question. "So, have you made contact yet?"

Sometimes Teague hated being right. Again, he asked himself why it mattered that Marsh was only here about the favor he'd promised. It would be wiser to ask himself why this particular woman had brought Marsh to ask favors at all.

"Not yet. Why, is our Miss McClure getting antsy already?"

"Dr. McClure."

Teague didn't react. "I told you before that this wouldn't be simple. I'll let her know when it's time."

"But you can get her in?"

Teague's sixth sense kicked in. He was careful to keep his demeanor the same as he'd cultivated over the last year, that of the wastrel black sheep, member of one of Boudry Parish's wealthiest families who didn't give a good damn about what anyone thought of him. He'd been a natural for the part.

"Yeah, I'll get her in."

Marsh smiled. "Thanks. I really appreciate your help on this."

Marshall's smile seemed easy and sincere, but the

skin on the back of Teague's neck still itched. "What, is there a promotion in this for you if she finds the cure for cancer out there in the bayou or something?"

Marsh laughed. "You know Sullivan money only buys political offices, not tenure. But I will say this is a real boon to our university, and it won't hurt me any to be the one to facilitate Dr. McClure's research while she's here."

"I'd never even heard of the field before you mentioned it."

"She's made quite a name for herself, both on her own and with the extensive research she did with her father when he was alive. He's a legend. Sort of the Indiana Jones of the botany field."

Teague heard the words, but he was more interested in watching Marsh's face. His half brother enjoyed his work. That Marshall had been strong enough to follow his own path was something Teague admired the hell out of. It was the one true bond he felt he had with him.

As children, their father had made Teague's life a living hell. But Marsh hadn't had it easy either, despite appearances to the contrary.

Not that he'd ever appreciated Teague's attempts to help him out. Teague had always been amused by the fact that ironically it was he, perhaps better than anyone else, who understood what Marsh had gone through.

After all, they were both bastards.

But Marsh hadn't thanked him for stepping in when they were kids, for using his fists when Marsh preferred to use his brains, and that independent streak had continued into adulthood. Perhaps for good reason. Marsh had ultimately gotten what he wanted.

Maybe Teague was reading more into this unusual request for help than actually existed. They were both adults. Perhaps Marshall was just trying to behave as if they were a normal family.

It was all Teague could do not to choke on the thought.

"I'll contact her just as soon as the time is right," he said shortly.

"Thanks, Teague. I really do appreciate it." Tension filled the short silence that followed, until Marsh rose, absently brushing at his pants.

"Sure you can't stay for a beer?" Teague had no idea where that came from, except that he suddenly didn't want to sever this new bond. Stupid. He'd made it a policy not to offer anything of himself to anyone. Ever. He did what he did because he wanted to. No one owed him. He owed no one.

Except Grand-mère. And soon even that debt would be paid. If it ever truly could be.

"No, I have to get back."

Teague swallowed the sigh of relief and ignored the small sense of hurt in the easy rejection. Like he said, stupid.

Stupid to want. Even more foolish to need.

The silence spun out a bit awkwardly, and Teague sensed Marshall wasn't quite sure how to end the conversation either. Teague noticed his fingers curling into his hand. *Against the impulse to shake hands?*

Teague's own fingers tightened into fists beneath the desk. "Yeah, another time maybe."

Now it was Marshall's turn to look relieved. "Sure."

And then he was gone.

Teague stared at the doorway, hating the empty feeling inside his chest.

Swearing harshly, he yanked up the phone. He was here to do a job. Nothing else. Including getting mixed up with his half brother and a wild-haired scientist.

One job. After that he'd never have to step foot in Bruneaux or Louisiana again.

Erin rubbed the grit from her eyes as she opened the door to her apartment. Another all-nighter at the campus lab, and archives had turned up nothing she hadn't already documented. Not that she'd expected it to. But she wouldn't be a responsible scientist if she didn't examine all of the data the college had collected.

And, boy, were they avid collectors. She had been fascinated by the firsthand recounting of various *Rada* and *Petro* ceremonies dating as far back as the late 1800s. The reactions of some of the participants in these wild, untamed rituals had varied. But she had no new insights as to what caused the responses. At least nothing pharmacological.

She knew from experience in Haiti and Africa with her father years ago that it would be next to impossible to get the local initiates, or *hounsis*, as the followers of the voudoun religion were called, to agree that there was a scientific reason for participants' ability to perform such seemingly impossible feats during their rituals.

Mac had been convinced, as were others before him, that there was a medical reason for this. And after their extensive research, Erin had become fascinated by the possibilities as well.

But she wasn't there to convince the *hounsis*, or change their perspective on their religion. She would come to her own scientific conclusions. They were free to agree or disagree with her findings. All she needed from them was trust, to share with her the specific plants and derivatives used in these ceremonies.

"And my ticket in is a bad-tempered Cajun with a gun," she muttered as she dumped her file-stuffed backpack on the chair inside the door. She groaned in relief.

"I didn't bring the gun tonight, *ange*," came a dark voice from the depths of her apartment.

Erin froze for a split second. That voice had plagued her thoughts for almost a week. Thoughts that hadn't always been about their business relationship. She tried to tell herself that the thrill stealing over her was due to her anticipation of what her visitor might have come to tell her about seeing the *mambo*. But at four in the morning, she doubted it.

"Hiding out from another jealous husband, Comeaux?"

He chuckled, a sexy, dangerous sound that vibrated in the hot air. Her pulse instantly went into overdrive. No doubt the man had perfect night vision; nocturnal predators often did. Or she'd have been tempted to slither into the chair—with or without her backpack still on it.

Wait a minute. Hot air. It was hot in here. Again.

Without benefit of the light, she stalked to the air conditioner.

"Off. You turned off my air." She swung toward the direction the voice had come from earlier. Her bed.

She could barely make out the shadowed sprawl that was him. Against her will, she'd pictured him on that very bed many times. He was far more dominating a presence there than she'd ever imagined. He filled her bed to overflowing . . . just as he had her tub.

Just as he would you, her little voice whispered.

"I'm used to the heat, *mon ange*." There was a pause. "I like it."

Feeling herself sinking fast, Erin shook herself free of the spell his seductive voice was weaving around her. "Well, I'm not. I have spent the best part of the last several hours fantasizing about my nice cool room and my nice cool shower."

"The shower is available, *chèr*."

Her eyes adjusted to the dark, and she could see the white flash of his teeth in the slant of moonlight. His tone made it clear he didn't consider the bed off limits to her either.

The feel of his hands on her skin was still a vivid memory. So clear she swore she could feel them right now. Warm, slightly rough, gently firm, demanding, taking.

Swallowing tightly, she squeezed her eyes shut, but

it was no defense against the mental image of his mouth coming closer to hers.

During the last week of long hours, she'd spent too much time thinking about Teague. He roused in her too many conflicting thoughts, too many unsettling emotions. But one thing was clear. Any time spent with him on . . . unbusinesslike pursuits, would be a mistake. She'd fought too long and too hard to waste one precious moment or one hard earned cent on anything but her study.

And that meant the only invitation she was accepting from him was to meet the *mambo.*

"Well, if you think it's safe for you to be on the streets, then I'd appreciate it if you'd leave me to take a shower alone for a change."

"I wasn't planning on joining you."

Erin felt her cheeks heat, knowing she'd asked for that one. Why did his teasing make such a direct hit on her female ego? She'd never really thought she had one.

Maybe that was why. What he made her body feel had nothing to do with science or basic function. He made her feel utterly female. He made her ache.

No man had ever made her ache.

She straightened her shoulders.

"This time," he added.

Oh, boy.

"But if you want to cool off, then do it now."

"I beg your pardon?" she demanded, taken aback by his sudden command. "I realize you have no respect for my privacy, but if you think you can just—"

"Erin."

That one word brought her little speech to a shuddering halt.

Her name on his lips. So simple. And yet her body had leapt in response to that single, softly spoken word. "What?"

She heard the bed springs groan under his weight as he moved. He came off the bed and moved toward her, the action fluid and graceful, like that of a sleek black panther she'd once seen, moving through the night, intent on one thing. Cornering its prey.

Without meaning to, she backed up a step. Her thighs pressed against the cold radiator, her back against the air conditioner.

"Why are you here? What do you want?" she asked as he loomed in front of her.

He paused. His dark features were cast in the stark light of the moon, making him seem hard and chiseled. More like cold marble than warm man.

"Don't ask me what I want."

Erin straightened, drawn to the thread of uncertainty she heard in his voice.

"I just might tell you." Rough, almost hoarse. This time the intent was clear. Heat. Sexual heat.

"Teague, I—" She stopped short when she heard the same longing note in her own voice.

Suddenly he stepped back, the shadows swallowing him up once again. When he spoke this time he was near the door to the hall.

"Get a shower and put on something cool. I'm here to take you to the *mambo*. Now."

FOUR

Less than ten minutes later, dressed in fresh clothes and a scowl, Erin climbed into Teague's truck. His ancient truck.

Sweat formed on her upper lip and across her forehead. She didn't have to look at the dash to know there would be no air-conditioning. She closed the rattling door and yanked the seat belt across her lap. "At least something works in here," she grumbled.

Erin felt him climb in, and the cab grew hotter. Talk about body heat. Erin didn't look at him. Her pulse hadn't quite recovered from that brief but intense moment they'd just shared in her room. No. She couldn't think about that now. Ever.

She forced her mind to the night's turn of events. She was exhausted by the long day, and now wired with the confusing energy Teague's nearness provoked in her . . . This was not the way she'd planned to take what would probably be the single most important step in her study. Making first contact.

She shot Teague a covert glance and tried to ignore the trickle of sweat wending its way down between her breasts. As usual, he was calling the shots.

For now, she amended silently.

Erin fully intended to make the most of this encounter with the voodoo priestess. If she played her cards right, she might be able to gain enough of the *mambo*'s trust to eliminate the middle man. Then Teague would be out of the picture for good.

She felt his gaze shift to her at that exact moment.

"Don't get any bright ideas, *chèr*."

He'd spoken softly, the words barely drifting to her across the quiet space of the truck cab . . . yet they were no less menacing than if he'd held a gun to her head and shouted them.

Damn the man, anyway. He was too perceptive by half. "I can take care of myself." Mac may not have been a traditional parent, but he had seen to that. The realization that she didn't always appreciate it did little to soothe her nerves.

"You want to get back out of the swamp, you do what I say, when I say." There was not so much as a hint of the teasing Cajun bad boy she'd discovered naked in her tub. This man was all dark shadows and uncompromising edges.

She kept her gaze trained firmly out the side window, ignoring the slight tremor his words ignited inside her. "Just introduce me to the priestess. I can take it from there."

Teague glanced at her again. She felt it as strongly as if he'd touched her. "Until I say otherwise, you'll take it where I lead, Erin. Don't ever forget that."

Shifting uncomfortably, she remained silent as he wove his way through the waning moonlit side streets to the outskirts of the small town.

Teague turned onto a narrow, deeply rutted road. The truck bounced hard over the rough terrain until they were several miles into the woods. He finally—mercifully—brought the truck to a stop by a small half-rotted pier that listed drunkenly into a small bayou.

The headlights didn't penetrate too far into the shadows. She could make out only the dock and the glint of water beyond. Then Teague shut off the engine.

For a spine-chilling moment it was pitch-dark and stone quiet. Erin rubbed her hands along her thighs in an absent gesture. She heard a dull thudding sound and realized with a start that it was her heart.

In the sudden deafening silence she became almost excruciatingly aware of the man seated next to her. Her skin prickled, the hair on the back of her neck lifted, her mouth went dry, and her nipples tightened.

There was danger in the air. She knew it with an instinct honed over her twenty-nine years. Felt it. Tasted it.

And it didn't lie somewhere ahead in the deep of the bayou.

The danger that she faced was right there in the truck.

The most frightening realization of all was that the danger wasn't Teague. It was her.

"Where are—" Her words came out deep and throaty. She stopped short and swallowed. Had she ever sounded like that?

The confusing yet exquisite sensations skittered along her body, filtered into her mind, diluting everything until the only research she could concentrate on was discovering why he made her feel like this. And what could be done about it. And when.

"This is Bayou Bruneaux." His voice slid into the silence between them. "We'll take my bateau from here."

Bayou Bruneaux. Cajun translation: "dark waters."

Oh, the waters were dark all right . . . and getting deeper every second.

Did he have any idea how overly sensitized she was to the sound of just his voice? Her face burned in the dark of the cab, but her mind persisted down its chosen path.

"Fine." She didn't dare say more. The only thing worse than this sudden overwhelming awareness of him . . . and of herself . . . would be him knowing it and tossing it back in her face.

When she was on solid ground—both real and mental—then she could face whatever he chose to throw at her.

Or at least she told herself she could. It was the only thing she had to hold on to right now. To help her get past this moment. And on to the next one. And the next one, until Teague didn't have this effect on her anymore. Until just looking at him didn't make her think of sweaty nights and cool cotton sheets and his hands on her . . . the parts of her that ached, and the ones still yet to.

Until she could do something, anything, to get him gone.

Erin grabbed her tote and crawled quickly out of the cab. The clanging sound of the door rang like a shot over the still waters. If it was possible, the air here was even thicker, steamier. She didn't mind the perspiration rolling off her now. . . . Maybe she could sweat out the heat he stirred in her.

"Careful," he warned. "The dock isn't stable."

That isn't the only thing that isn't stable. He was too close behind her. She moved a bit faster, wanting to get on with it. She focused on that, allowing the excitement of what lay ahead to creep into her veins. The seductive thrum of entering a situation where the quantities were unknown. . . .

But most of all she didn't want him to touch her.

The dark seduction of his unknown quantities would have to remain unexplored.

There was only one boat tied to the rotting wood. The small bateau looked as old as Teague's truck. She didn't say a word, just carefully lowered herself down, then sat on the front seat. Teague moved silently behind her, barely dipping the boat as he shifted his weight to switch on the small electric motor.

The low, putt-putting sound hardly disturbed the heavy air.

They moved slowly out into the water. As Erin's

eyes adjusted, she saw that the bayou was narrow where they'd docked but quickly opened into a wider path. She could make out the bald cypress crowding the shoreline, their knobby roots bending into the murky waters like spider legs.

Surprisingly, the silence between them became almost easy. Almost. Erin purposely put her mind to what she wanted to accomplish. Teague hadn't let her bring her sample kits or a camera. But she'd tucked a minirecorder in her tote, along with a notebook.

"Don't get your hopes up, Erin." His voice was hardly more than a whisper. She heard him clearly, acutely.

Her careful mental preparations fled, blurred as that seductive veil drifted over her again, unwanted, but there nonetheless. Hopes . . . Hers had always centered on her work. But right now her thoughts, her hopes, were anything but professional.

"You may not get a chance to meet her this time," he went on. "Tonight we are observers. This is a public ritual, but still very closely monitored."

"Then why the restriction on the camera?" she asked. "I would have been discreet. And I would never use anything I took without full permission. But in order to document their—"

"You'll have to do this my way. Or no way."

Irritation bristled through her, and she welcomed the feeling. It helped her to focus. "Why don't we let Belisaire be the judge of what is and isn't acceptable? If she'd said no, I would have kept the camera packed."

"Or just out of sight."

She spun to face him. "How dare you question my ethics?"

His hair glowed blue black in the fading moonlight, his features cast in shadow. He looked huge . . . powerful. An irresistible invitation to play on the dark side.

To her dismay, another chill shot down her spine.

She held firmly—desperately—to her indignation. A clear-cut, easy emotion. "I won't defend myself to you. You shouldn't judge people you don't know."

When he simply stared at her, she grew uncomfortable. Indignation became agitation . . . not all of it unpleasurable. Frowning, not caring if he saw it as surrender, she turned back around and crossed her arms under her breasts.

After several long nerve-racking moments, a low chuckle floated to her. Sexy, soft.

The naked bad boy in the tub had returned. With an annoyingly tempting vengeance. She wanted to groan out loud, to beg him to stop doing this to her.

"I think knowing you any better could be dangerous, *chèr*."

"You don't know the half of it," she muttered under her breath. And dear God help her if he decided he wanted to.

The boat came around a long lazy bend and Erin saw flickering lights in the trees ahead.

Minutes later as she was stepping from the bateau to the dock, he leaned in close from behind her and whispered, "But that's the half that's the most fun, *ange*."

She almost fell out of the boat.

His hands clamped on her hips and lifted her up to

the dock, then were gone almost before she could register their latent strength.

"Watch that first step, *chèr*," he added softly. "It's always the hardest one to take."

Intelligent, stubborn, confident, mouthy, independent, worldly. And yet no idea how sexy she really was. In a word, trouble.

"Watch out, Erin McClure," he warned too softly for her to hear. "You have no idea what you just walked into."

He followed her down the path in front of them, swearing at the problems she was causing him, and all the ones she had yet to. He had a sinking sensation that his warning applied just as much to himself.

She stopped at the edge of the clearing. "I hear drums." The sound of a distant rhythmic pounding, almost more pulse than beat, was clearly distinguishable from the sounds of the bayou's night creatures.

"The ceremony isn't over. Those are the *cata* and *seconde*. The *maman* drums haven't even started yet." Teague circled her and headed toward an almost indistinguishable track cut into the cypress. "Follow me."

She saluted him sharply, then did a little obeisant roll of the hand from forehead to waist as she bowed.

Teague bit back the surprise bark of laughter. So he was used to giving orders. Both at the Eight Ball and in his work as a U.S. Customs investigator.

But he wouldn't apologize. With Erin, it was probably best, for both their sakes, to keep her a bit annoyed with him.

She swept a hand in front of her. "Well?" she said sharply. "What are we waiting for?"

Which apparently wouldn't be a problem, he added, turning away as the smile curved his lips.

But as he pushed deeper into the dense growth, the image of her face when she'd turned to him in the bateau came too clearly to mind. The moon had glowed white on her, highlighting her spiky halo of hair, illuminating her upturned face. Something had moved inside him then.

Her indignation was clear, in her voice and her expression, but so was something else. Something he'd fought seeing, fought hearing . . . but had remained burned in his mind's eye.

Want.

There had been such a deep wealth of want in those eyes of hers. To say nothing of that hollow ache he'd heard in her voice earlier, before she'd wisely shut up.

His body had heard it, had responded loud and clear. The memory of walking up to her in the apartment assaulted him, catching him with his guard down, punching a big hole in his control.

He'd meant to intimidate, calculated his moves to ensure his control of the situation, control of her . . . all part of his job, one he was very good at. He hadn't counted on getting caught in the web too. Had barely backed away before becoming hopelessly caught in its sticky, destructive strands.

Too much was at stake.

Want . . .

Worse than the most addictive drug.

Right up there with need and hope. Individually they were dangerous. Combined they were soul destroyers.

Teague pushed down the path. Best to get on with it. He had to get Erin set up, then do some quick business while he was out there. Risky, but the situation was as controlled as he could make it. He had no guarantees for later. And he didn't need both Marsh and Erin breathing down his neck.

"Can you tell me what it is we're observing tonight?"

She moved so silently behind him, her words were the only sound that reached his ears. That earned her another measure of his respect. He knew firsthand how difficult that was, especially out here. That skill had meant the difference between life and death for him more times than he cared to count. The fact that she was doing it and keeping pace with him told him it was an ability so ingrained as to be second nature.

Good thing. Depending on how his meeting went later tonight, she might be needing it for more than observing voodoo rituals undetected.

The idea of Erin in mortal danger didn't sit at all well with him. And that realization sat even worse.

He shook it off. Erin claimed she could take care of herself. And Teague believed her. A more self-reliant woman he'd never met. Except perhaps the one they were on their way to see.

Another smile curved his lips. It hadn't occurred to

him until now, but if Belisaire chose to make an appearance, it just might make taking on Marsh's favor worth all the pain-in-the-butt adjustments he'd had to make in this case.

"Teague?"

His skin actually prickled in awareness at the sound of his name on her lips. Not a good sign, Comeaux.

"You'll see when you get there," he said. "If we get a move on, you might be able to witness the end of the ritual. She might speak with you afterward. No guarantees."

"I'm surprised. Grateful, but surprised. Mac and I had to work months and months in Africa before we could so much as witness a meeting between the *bokor* there and an individual seeking advice. We were never permitted to observe an actual ritual ceremony. They had no public ones at that time."

"Yeah, well, let's just say I have an inside track."

He felt the warmth of her hand the instant before she placed it on his arm. He stopped suddenly and she walked right into him. Her breast, feeling soft and fuller than he remembered from that night in her bathroom, pressed hard into his arm.

Her soft gasp made his jaw clench. She backed away from him, but he doubted his body would register that fact for several hours.

"Sorry," she said. "I, uh, I just wanted to let you know that, despite our unusual beginning, I really do appreciate all you're doing for me."

Something in her voice pulled at him and he found himself looking at her before he was aware of it. As he did, he realized what it was. Uncertainty. A trait he'd have thought Erin McClure didn't possess.

One he was disturbed to discover he had a trace of as well.

"It's a favor to Marshall. That's all." He turned and continued down the narrow trail.

"What is your connection to Marshall? He's never said. I don't know him that well, but I admit I was a bit surprised to—"

Teague caught her by the forearms and held her still.

"Surprised someone like him had a connection with someone like me?" He hated the dark emotions simmering inside him, but he was helpless against them. Just as he was apparently helpless against all the other emotions Dr. Erin McClure aroused in him. "Is that what you meant, chèr?"

He'd startled her, he knew. She didn't try to pull away, nor did she appear angry. But her pulse under his fingertips told another story. He felt his blood begin to stir hot and heavy, like the night air, pushing thick and hard through his veins.

His hold on her changed. He still held her captive, yet now she held him too, in her own way. He couldn't stop touching her.

No moon filtered through the trees. Her eyes were black, bottomless, but he didn't have to see them to know she was responding to him. He could feel it, pulsing under his fingers, beating in his ears, thrumming in his groin. He could smell it. Wanted badly to taste it.

His hands slid up her arms to her shoulders. He

exerted just enough pressure for her to know he wanted her closer but didn't wait and stepped in closer himself.

"Erin."

"I've never met anyone like you," she said on a shaky whisper.

The admission shot a hot thrill through him. "What am I like, *chèr?*"

She stared at him, her face cast in deep shadow. The silence between them stretched out, the only sound that of the earthy throb of the *maman* drums as they echoed through the trees. Teague felt that beat deep inside his belly, and lower.

Just when he thought she wouldn't answer, she spoke.

"Dangerous. To me."

"Why? What do you think I'm going to do to you, Erin?"

There was a pause, then her voice stroked him again. "It's not what I think you'll do, it's what I want you to do."

"What is that, Erin?" He took another irreversible step forward and lowered his mouth close to hers. "What do you want me to do to you, Erin? Tell me." He brushed his lips against hers. "Tell me."

"Teague." His name was no more than a gasp.

"That's right, *ange.*" He touched his lips to hers. "Say my name again."

"I don't—"

He kissed her then, slowly, completely, swallowing words he should probably hear but didn't want to. She stilled. He took the kiss deeper, pressing his tongue past her soft lips, twining it with hers. Not admitting, even now, that he was inside her mouth, pulling her body tight against his, that it might go beyond that. That *he* wanted it to.

When she lifted her hands to his arms, grasping his biceps, digging her fingertips into the twitching muscles there, he felt something drop hard into his stomach, leaving him almost light-headed. Lighthearted.

Something beyond sexual pleasure, beyond the carnal knowledge of her that his body was screaming for.

She leaned into him and relaxed her mouth, granting him an invitation, one he took to heart.

And that is exactly why he pulled away.

They stood staring at each other, their breathing audible in the small space between them. Teague felt something shift inside him. Around him. As if this moment somehow defined a very important change in the world. That nothing would ever be the same.

"He's my half brother."

Erin was obviously as nonplussed by his declaration as he was for blurting it out.

"Who is?"

He could still taste her on his tongue, felt her there as he spoke. It made his skin heat and his body even harder. "Marshall. You asked what my connection is to him."

He waited while she absorbed that information. It was common knowledge in the parish; she would have heard anyway. He was surprised she hadn't just asked Marsh. But somehow him telling her was like a declaration. Of what, he was afraid to ask himself.

"Are you close?"

Her question took him by surprise. She'd asked sincerely, honest interest clear in her tone. He wondered if she'd forgotten she was holding his arms. He hadn't forgotten anything.

"No."

Silence fell heavily between them. Her gaze dropped to where she touched him. He felt her fingers tense on his skin, then she carefully relaxed her grip and let her hands fall away.

Only when she moved back enough to put pressure on his own hold, did he find the will to drop his hands as well.

"This is the first thing he's asked me for in a very long time."

"Well, I'm grateful he asked, and more grateful you agreed. Whatever your reasons."

He didn't want her gratitude. But that begged the question of just what it was he did want. He refused to think about that.

His reasons for being here, for bringing her here, precluded his ever answering that question.

"We'd better move."

At that instant the drums stopped. The sudden cessation of the beat, the final echo through the trees, froze them both momentarily in place.

Before Teague could move, the underbrush rustled to his left. Without thought he turned toward the noise and pulled Erin behind him. There was a whisper of sound, then in the next instant, they were surrounded by at least a dozen *hounsis*, all dressed in white cotton shifts. The glow of their clothes against the dark background was surreal, almost otherworldly.

Erin tugged at the arm he'd wrapped around her, trying to step past him. He turned and pulled her forward, so they were side by side, staring down the silent wraiths.

"Initiates?" Erin whispered.

"Yes. Followers of Belisaire," Teague answered back, keeping his voice low.

She looked at him, then turned back as the trees rustled once again. A small figure eased into view, almost as if she had been part of the trees, but now stood separate, alone. Also dressed in white, the woman was small, both in height and build. But the power radiating from her was almost palpable.

"Teague." The woman's voice was strong, commanding, and, he knew, surprising to those who had never heard it before.

He glanced down at Erin, needing to see her reaction, as if it would somehow make everything that was to come understandable. He knew it wouldn't. And yet he didn't—couldn't—look away. The only time in his life he'd known Belisaire's presence not to hold his full attention.

The creeping dawn helped to illuminate Erin's face. Avid curiosity and sharp awareness lit her eyes. Her even expression couldn't hide the almost tangible excitement he swore he felt growing in her. Strange, hypnotic.

Teague worked hard to shake the unsettling feeling.

"Belisaire is the *mambo*." He turned to face the woman. She did nothing but stand there, yet she commanded the attention of all those in the clearing. Including Erin.

"She is also my *grand-mère* Comeaux."

FIVE

Erin swung her gaze to Teague. "Your grandmother?"

"Yes, Dr. McClure," Belisaire answered for him.

Erin turned back to her. The woman had somehow managed to close the distance between them without a sound. She stuck out her hand. "I'm very honored to meet you."

Belisaire studied her proffered hand, then laid her small dark-skinned hand over Erin's. The slow scrutiny of her black-eyed gaze was more than a bit unsettling. Erin had been subjected to examinations before, by chieftains of little-known aboriginal tribes, leaders of warriors in countries still more untamed than civilized. None had made her feel so exposed. She felt naked to her soul.

After what felt like hours, but was certainly only seconds, the priestess lifted her hand and spoke. "You have faced the darkness before, Erin McClure. You will face it again. Here."

"Yes," Erin answered. "I am very grateful for the opportunity."

A smile split the woman's dark features, rocking Erin with its unexpected whiteness. Here was Teague's grandmother in the smile they both shared. And, Erin realized, the darkness that lay beneath the blinding smile.

"I hope you still feel that way when your time here is done." The woman turned slightly, as if to leave, then stopped. "But be warned, Erin McClure. The darkness I spoke of isn't what we do here in the bayous in the full of the moon. It resides in you and one other. Make no mistake, Erin McClure. The choice will be yours. May you both find the light."

This time she faced Teague, completely shutting Erin out. Belisaire lifted her hand to caress the side of his face as one would a small boy. So incongruous to the woman of a second ago, so . . . grandmotherly . . .

"It takes too much to bring you to me," she said to Teague, who stood still under her touch.

Erin was captivated by the notion of Teague being raised by this woman.

"But this time I forgive your long absence." She dropped her hand to his and covered it tightly.

Teague leaned down and kissed her cheek. "You forgive too much, Grand-mère." He grinned. "And I'll always let you."

The older woman smiled in return, then her features tightened, and just like that Belisaire the *mambo* was back. Teague straightened, but she held his hand.

"You will have a choice to make too, *chèr*. My only guidance is to trust your heart. It is time."

Her whispered words were meant for Teague alone and just barely reached Erin's ears.

"The only heart I have belongs to you alone, Grand-mère."

She dropped his hand with a sharp snap. "Then you are already lost."

Teague's smile vanished, and his voice dropped to a rough whisper. "Are you just now accepting that, Grand-mère?"

She just turned and walked away, melting back into the trees like a wraith. Erin looked around and realized she and Teague were alone once again. Or were they?

She shivered. "Quite a woman, your *grand-mère*."

"And at times a real pain in the ass," Teague muttered.

Erin was dying to ask him a hundred questions about the older woman, not one of them having to do with her research. "I take it the evening's festivities are over?"

Teague turned his attention to her. Erin felt it like a live thing, touching her.

"No. We follow. The invitation has been issued."

Erin laughed. "Then I guess it is a good thing you're along. I never would have deciphered that as an invitation."

Teague didn't respond. He simply studied her for several seconds, the heat creeping back into his dark eyes.

It filled her just as swiftly.

He stepped closer. She didn't move.

"Your first choice is now, Erin."

She curled her fingers into her palms against the sudden need to touch him. To connect with him in a physical way, as if that could diminish or explain the connection she felt with him on an entirely different plane.

"And what is that?"

"Follow me into the swamp. To Belisaire. Enter my world."

Erin shivered. It was a delicious sensation she didn't want to stop. She wanted him to touch her, run his hands over her sensitized skin, prolong it.

"Or?" She struggled to keep her voice even.

"Walk away, Erin. There are things you don't understand."

"That's precisely why I am here, Teague. To understand."

"I'm not talking about voodoun rituals and plant medicine."

"Well, that's the only thing I'm talking about." If he believed the lie, then maybe she could too.

"Your decision is made then." It wasn't a question.

"It was made long before I met you, Teague. I have to do this."

"Already ignoring Belisaire's advice. I learned long ago the folly of doing that. She is never wrong."

"I *want* to do this. My *choice*." She stepped back, a clear statement of her independence. "My responsibility as well."

He studied her for another long moment, then turned and walked away. "Follow me."

She did. And it was both the most difficult and the easiest thing she'd ever done.

Teague watched, bemused, as Erin entered the small house Belisaire used as her *hounfour*, her center for worship and healing. There were a lot of memories tied up in that house. The summer after his mother took her life, it had been his refuge. When he didn't get his act together fast enough to suit Belisaire, it became his prison. Confinement he'd desperately wished had been solitary. Not filled with people who wandered in and out at all hours of the day and night. He'd spent many a night in the small airless second-floor room, plotting his escape. From his father, from Belisaire, from Bruneaux.

Belisaire had eventually prevailed. Teague stayed in school. Stayed out of trouble. Or at least made damn sure he didn't get caught. The only thing she'd never gotten him to do was see his father again.

And, after four years, at age eighteen, Teague had escaped.

Now, more than a decade later, he was back. The woman who had saved his life at fourteen was in trouble, whether she believed herself to be or not.

"Stubborn old lady," Teague muttered under his breath, but there was more than a trace of affection and respect in his tone. She'd long ago earned both. The door closed behind Erin. Teague shook off the curiosity, the need to stay and observe how these two women who so fascinated him dealt with one another.

That he felt so certain Erin would hold her own with Belisaire made him smile even as it made him uncomfortable.

But he had no time for this. He shut off thoughts of Erin stepping into this part of his life, a part no one in his new life knew about, and turned them to the reason he'd come here tonight.

He quickly disappeared into the trees until he came to a small dilapidated boathouse that was more of a covered mooring. He stepped inside, smelled the cigarette smoke, and breathed a small sigh of relief.

"Skeeter, what do you have for me?"

Erin stepped from the porch, nodding politely as several white-clad men and women walked past her into the small house. Apparently this was a common occurrence at any hour.

She paused several feet into the clearing and breathed deeply. Thick and heavy with the scent of the bayou, it actually felt good. Maybe she'd get used to being here after all. A grin spread across her face and she gave in to the urge to hug herself. The meeting with Belisaire had gone better than expected. So much so that Erin could barely contain her excitement. Belisaire understood what Erin's interests were and was willing, on her own terms, to help her. In fact, she'd made the whole meeting seem preordained, as if it were her idea.

It was far more than she'd hoped for or had ever

thought to gain this early on. She bit down on the triumphant laugh and looked around. Teague. She had to find him. Thank him.

Much of her success that morning had to be due to his influence. Belisaire hadn't specifically said so, but it had been clear to Erin by some of the questions the priestess asked her that Teague bringing her here had carried great weight.

The excitement running through her changed . . . the wild hum turned darker, sweeter. Erin worked hard to shake off the temptation to explore why Belisaire was so interested in her thoughts on Teague. The older woman wore her mantle of power like a visible cloak. And Erin had quickly discovered she was incapable of not answering any question Belisaire posed to her. As if she'd been compelled.

She'd told herself she complied as a means of establishing trust. But sitting in the shadowed peristyle, the roofed courtyard Belisaire used as her *bagi*, her innermost sanctum, Erin knew she was not the one in control.

A sudden shiver raced over her, making her rub her arms.

She closed the disquieting train of thought. She was here as a scientist and tonight she had had great success. Personal revelations didn't play a part in her role here. She'd be wise to get that straight in her head right now.

To that end, she moved toward the edge of the woods, near the trail she and Teague had taken to this spot. She'd find him, thank him for his help, and ask to be taken home. She needed to sleep. Tomorrow would bring long hours of transcribing the taped conversation Belisaire had approved.

"Teague?" She kept her voice low. The only sounds she heard were the muted cries of the nutria and other night creatures. She stepped a few feet down the path and called his name again. Nothing.

She thought about going all the way back to the bateau, but even with her exceptional navigational skills, she wasn't foolish enough to enter the tangled web of trees on her own. Teague had spent the better part of his childhood here, knew these trails blindfolded.

Erin found it impossible not to give in to her curiosity about her guide, his intriguing past, and the knowledge he must have of the voodoo practices in this area. She didn't even bother telling herself her interest was strictly scientific.

A rustling sound about ten yards to her left, then men's muted voices, caught her attention. She walked in that direction and discovered a small trail cut into the dense stand of oak and gum trees. She'd gone several steps before she realized it wasn't Teague's voice she heard.

"It has to be here by Sunday!"

The heated whisper had Erin stumbling to a halt. Not sure whether to make her presence known or simply to retreat, she ended up hearing more.

"I'm trying, dammit." This voice was louder, deeper than the first one. Both carried an accent. Caribbean. Haitian maybe. Or something close.

"It's not my fault the damn boat got caught in that tropical depression offshore."

"Well, I have it set on my end. Unless you want to be gator bait, you get it here by Sunday. Because if Customs noses in and I go down on this, I take you with me."

Without realizing it, Erin backed slowly into the trees off the path. Her heart was pounding. Drug trafficking? Or something just as illegal. She was sure of it.

Only one man emerged onto the path. Short, slight of build, and dressed in the same white cotton pants and tunic as everyone else she'd seen tonight. Damn. Not much of a description.

For what, Erin? That stopped her cold. What *was* she planning to do? Run to the local sheriff? Bring local and possibly federal law enforcement attention here? Belisaire would shut down all communication in a heartbeat as soon as she learned Erin had made the initial call.

Belisaire. Erin swallowed. This was her property. Was she in on this? And what about—No. This didn't involve her. Whatever those men had planned was none of her business. She was here to observe, to learn. Not get in the middle of a drug war.

She waited several more minutes, until she was sure she was alone, then stepped from her hiding place.

And directly into Teague's unyielding chest.

He balanced her weight against him by holding her shoulders. "What are you doing out here, Erin?" The demand was cold and unflinching.

"Looking for you." She wanted to move out of his grasp, but didn't.

"Well, you found me. Now let's get the hell out of here."

Something about the way he said it, or maybe the way he scanned the area around them, made Erin uneasy.

Just where had he been? What had he been doing back here?

"Where does this path lead anyway?" The question sounded far from casual, so she was surprised when he answered her.

"To a boathouse another half mile past where we docked."

She looked from the path to him. "Then why didn't we dock there?"

"Belisaire was occupied earlier. She asked that we come in from the front." Teague didn't bat an eyelash.

So why was Erin almost positive he was lying? Or not telling her the whole truth?

But since when did he owe her whole truths? Especially as they applied to himself?

And why was it those were precisely the truths she most wanted to know?

Erin stepped back, out of his grasp. "I overheard a conversation tonight." She was operating on pure instinct, not of a scientist but a woman.

"Is that so?" He held her gaze steadily, the mask so complete she couldn't read anything in his expression. "Is that how you research? Hide behind bushes and eavesdrop?"

"Hardly. Belisaire has been more than generous," she said, not allowing him to goad her off the subject. "I

wouldn't return her goodwill by spying on her followers."

"What did you hear, Erin?"

"Two men. Setting up a deal."

"What kind of deal?" Again, the same flat, emotionless tone. About as far away from the black sheep, heart-
breaker, pool hall entrepreneur as he could get.

Yet it wasn't until now that she felt as if she was
seeing the real man. Emotionless? Cold? Inviolable?

Erin repressed the shiver that raced over her skin.
On the surface, yes. But what she felt was heat. Intensity. A sharp focused energy that cut through everything
else.

And she somehow doubted he'd gotten all that from
shooting eight ball with a bunch of drunks.

Who are you really, Teague Comeaux?

Gambler? Thief? *Bokor?*

Drug dealer?

"What sort of deal, Erin?"

She studied his eyes and found herself telling him
the rest of it. "I'm not sure. I assume drugs or something else equally illegal. They were talking about boats
and shipping times and U.S. Customs getting in the
way."

Teague didn't react. And yet the air between them
suddenly sizzled with tension.

"Tell me what they said."

It was the sudden softening of his tone that had the
hair on her arms standing on end. This man was deadly.

The question was, Who would his target be? The
good guys?

Or the bad?

"Did you see either of them?"

It was too late to stop now. "I saw one of them. A man, short, dark skinned, wearing white cotton pants." She cut off his next words. "I know. That hardly narrows the field. But it's the best I can do. I couldn't see his face clearly enough even to guess his age. But I—"

"He didn't go back toward the house?"

"No." She pointed down the path she'd asked about earlier. "I guess he went to the boathouse."

Teague was silent for a moment, then he turned away, facing the way she'd come. "We'd better go. You have a lot of work to do later this morning, I imagine."

Erin felt like someone had just spun her hard on a merry-go-round. "Wait a minute. That's it? End of interrogation?"

"Well, it doesn't sound like you heard or saw enough to do anything about it."

"I could still contact the parish police."

She didn't realize she'd tossed that out as bait until he didn't take it.

"Fine. But I doubt they will do anything. There have been rumors of everything from drug running to white slavery rings being operated out of the swamps, *chèr*. Without any real evidence, your story wouldn't make the top third of the pile."

"But I know what I heard, what I saw."

"And I happen to know that all those rumors aren't rumors either."

"How is that?"

He stepped closer, blocking out the night and all of

her surroundings. "I grew up in the swamps. I know firsthand how dangerous it is out here." His accent deepened, all the more foreboding for the lazy way it sounded. "The gators out here aren't all the four-legged variety."

Her heart began to pound in her ears. "I told you before, Comeaux. I can take care of myself."

"And for the most part, *ange*, I believe that. Truly I do." He lifted a hand to her face, rubbed the side of his thumb down her cheek, the gesture meant to seduce rather than soothe.

It was working alarmingly well.

The man might be a drug dealer or gun runner, Erin. Tell my body that! She eased back a fraction, until she felt only the heat of his skin. It was almost as powerful as his touch. "Then let me do what I think is best. If what you say is true, why not tell the police? At least I'll know I reported it."

"Belisaire won't appreciate having that sort of attention drawn to her."

Is that your only concern here? she thought. "I know that, Teague. Trust me, I wouldn't do something I thought would compromise my study here if I didn't think it necessary."

He touched her face again, this time letting his thumb come to rest on her bottom lip.

"Be-besides which—" her voice broke and she swallowed hard, "if what you say is true . . ." The feeling of his warm skin on her lip as she spoke was driving her mad. Why didn't he move away? Why didn't she? "The rumors," she went on doggedly, thinking she was in far more danger now than she had been eavesdropping on drug runners. "I would—I imagine Belisaire has probably dealt with worse."

Dear God, he was still staring at her mouth.

"Teague, are you listening to anything I'm saying?" Her voice was a heated whisper now.

"Oh, yes, Erin. Yes, I am." He looked up. "Say it again."

"Beli—" She gulped when he pressed his thumb just a bit inside her mouth so it touched the tip of her tongue. "Belisaire—"

He shook his head slowly. "My name, Erin. Say it again."

A long sigh eased out of her, past her now tender lips and his wet thumb, and with it went whatever was left of her common sense. "Oh, Teague."

"*Mais yeah, chèr.*"

He slid his thumb in deeper, pressing the rough pad on her tongue. She swallowed, closing her mouth on it. Her heart was pounding hard, shooting blood to that aching place between her thighs, engorging the muscles there, forcing nerve endings painfully, exquisitely to life.

"That's it, *ange.* Taste me."

She drew her tongue over his finger. He groaned, low and soft.

Bull's-eye.

She pressed her thighs together, anything to ease the ache.

He crowded his hips against hers, moving her backward until her shoulders connected with the bark of a tree.

He braced one forearm over her head and slowly withdrew his thumb. Holding her gaze with the sheer force of his will, he slowly and very purposely slid his now shiny wet thumb into his own mouth. She closed her eyes.

"Open them, Erin."

She didn't. Couldn't. Not yet.

Then she felt his fingers brush past her cheek, into the short length of her hair, pressing gently against her skull as he eased her head back a bit. When his thumb, warm and damp, came to rest on her temple, she trembled.

"Erin."

He was close. So close.

She opened her eyes. "We shouldn't." Her voice was throaty, hoarse.

"Do you always do what you should, *chèr?*"

"Yes." Why did that sound pitiable instead of honorable?

He lowered his arm, his hand cupping the other side of her face, tilting her mouth up until their lips barely brushed. "But is that always what you want?"

"Teague." There was pleading in her tone. For what, she couldn't be sure at this point.

"Do you want to kiss me again, Erin? Taste me like I tasted you?"

"Just because I want—"

"Yes, want," he interrupted. "Want me, Erin."

"I do." Full admission. What had she done?

"Then take what you want."

Oh, God. "But—"

"Take my mouth, *ange*."

"I—"

"Take me."

SIX

Erin reached up and captured his head, pulling him in that last breathtaking millimeter of space. His lips were warm and pliant on hers. Too pliant.

A whimpering sound caught in her throat.

"Kiss me, Erin," he said against her lips. "Don't just give. Take."

Such a simple request. Yet, for her, profound. The idea that she could take what she wanted. Take him.

The power rush was almost overwhelming. No waiting to be wanted in order to feel it was okay to want the same things. To act on those wants.

Equal. That's what she felt. And it felt so damn good.

"Come here," she whispered, and tugged his head closer. She took his mouth slowly. God it was a beautiful mouth. Wide with that slightly fuller lower lip. Courtesan lips on a man. Sensual. So provocative. Made for pleasure. She took some for herself, gently pulling that lip into her mouth.

He groaned, the sound low and tight. It made her clench so hard she almost came right there.

"God, Teague," she gasped. But she still controlled the kiss. Trembling hard, she slid her tongue into his mouth and tasted him.

He tilted his head just a bit, pulling her tongue in deeper, then let his hands move to her hips.

Erin felt her knees weaken. Teague continued to accept her invasion of his mouth, but his hands slid around to hold her waist, pulling her hips away from the tree.

Erin's hands tightened on his scalp. She ached so badly.

When he pulled her hard up between his hips they both groaned. And then the kiss changed.

He began to take what he wanted. He gave her his tongue, the sweet pressure of his hips cradling hers.

Never, not once, had she felt anything remotely like this with a man. Until now. With Teague Comeaux.

He released her mouth. Breathing heavily, he lifted his head and looked at her.

Both of them stood there, in the growing dawn of Bayou Bruneaux, and stared at each other.

Erin wondered if he felt the same inescapable sense that nothing would ever be the same again.

"Erin—"

"We'd better go." Suddenly Erin was afraid. No, she was terrified. Of what he was about to say. What he might be feeling. Even more of what he had made her feel. "I've got to get back. And you—" He brushed his thumb over her still-damp lips and she shuddered as pleasure rocked her.

"Will taste you again, Erin McClure. And again."

"Teague." The pleading was there again. But this time she knew it was for escape. Her world was suddenly and very rapidly spinning out of control. She badly needed some time alone to sort things out.

She sensed he knew exactly what she was thinking. And she felt all the more naked and vulnerable for it. Without a word, he drew slowly away from her. But just as she let her breath ease out, he lifted the thumb that had traced her lips and pulled it in his mouth.

"Oh, God," she whispered.

"He won't help you here, *chèr*." He let his hand drop to his side and put more distance between them. "In the bayou, I'm your only hope." He turned and walked away.

Erin watched him, the strong line of his shoulders.

Was he salvation? Or sin.

She found she wanted him to be both.

"Did everything go well last night?"

It wasn't until Marshall dropped by the lab that Erin remembered the clandestine meeting she'd overheard the night before. Teague had completely dominated her thoughts since then.

She didn't like the suspicions that raised in her mind.

Tired and confused, Erin worked up a smile for

Marshall. "Better than I'd ever hoped. I take it you talked to Teague."

Marshall pulled out a lab stool and sat. As always, he looked expensively rumpled. Erin found herself looking for any similarity between the casual blond man sitting in front of her, and his dark intense half brother.

"No. But word travels fast in Bruneaux. Your visit to Belisaire has already made the rounds."

Erin raised her eyebrows in surprise, though she supposed she shouldn't be. "She's a fascinating person. I'm lucky to have her cooperation."

Marshall laughed, and for some reason, the sound was more chilling than warm. "Belisaire has her reasons for helping you I'm sure. She doesn't do anything without purpose."

She'd felt the same way. But her curiosity was piqued. What exactly was the history between these two men? And Belisaire. "Teague said she raised him. At least part of the time. Did you live with her too?"

He gave a short bark of laughter. "Heavens no." Suddenly restless, Marshall slid off the stool and paced to the door and back. His attention strayed, as if distracted by thoughts of the past. "She took Teague in after his mother committed suicide. She's his maternal grandmother. He even took the Comeaux name when Belisaire retained custody."

Her mind stuck on one word. "Suicide?"

"It was ruled one anyway. She was Belisaire's daughter through and through. Involved in God knows what out there while growing up. She might have lived in town, on the Sullivan estate, playing the charming hostess to Father's endless social affairs, but no one forgot where she came from. You can't escape the bayou. Or Belisaire's influence. So who knows what really happened?" He shrugged, as if it didn't matter, then began pacing again, picking up various implements littering the table and replacing them without really looking at them. "I'm surprised you haven't heard the story. It wouldn't take more than a question or two about Teague to any of the locals to get the whole grisly tale."

She tried not to let her sudden tension show. Carefully relaxing her fingers on the keys of her laptop computer, she turned her attention back to the monitor. "I'm here to research plants used in voodoun rituals, not your brother."

"Half."

Erin glanced up at him. Had she imagined the slight edge in his voice? "I take it you two aren't close then."

"We were never given a chance to be. Father married my mother less than a year after Teague's mother died. I was eleven, Teague was almost fifteen. He had already disappeared into the swamps by then."

"But you are half—" Erin stopped, knowing she should just get back to work. Marshall answered her anyway.

"Yes, we are. My father is my natural father." He smiled but it was empty of humor. "One thing we have in common, our bastard heritage. At least Father married them eventually." He didn't sound the least bit grateful about that.

Erin swallowed the questions begging to be asked.

"Obviously you have formed some sort of relationship as adults. You asked him to help me."

Marshall stopped abruptly. He turned and sank back onto the stool, looking suddenly tired. "He took off over ten years ago. The day he turned eighteen. No one knew where he went. Not even Belisaire, or at least that's what she always maintained. He's been back in Bruneaux for close to a year now, running the Eight Ball. I guess he plans to stay." He raked his hand through his already disheveled hair. "So, I figured it was time we both started acting like adults. When your program was proposed to us, I just acted on it. Worst he could have done was turn me down."

Somehow Erin knew Marshall had never doubted Teague would help him. Just as she knew that Marshall wasn't entirely comfortable with that fact. There was more going on here, obviously. And it was none of Erin's business.

"Well, if it's any help, I'm truly grateful to you for asking. I know now that without his introduction, I'd never have gotten in with Belisaire like I have."

Marsh's smile made him look more little boy than man. She wondered if Teague had ever looked like a little boy. Thinking of his tragic background, she doubted it.

"I can only imagine how the two of you got on. Though I'm sure having Teague there helped to diffuse the tension somewhat."

She thought of their enigmatic meeting in the woods. Belisaire's words rang in her ears. *Choices.* Erin tuned it out, as she had all day. "Actually she was charming." Erin smiled. "Though rather intense. Teague didn't stay."

Marshall's brows narrowed. "No?"

"It's okay. I think it actually went smoother that way."

"Yes, Teague can be . . ."

"Equally intense?"

"Quite." His smile faded. "He did stay to take you back out, didn't he?"

"I had to hunt him down, but yes." Without warning images of his body pressing hers against that tree, of his mouth coming closer, his heated words, assaulted her. She felt her face blush and she turned back to her computer. But not quickly enough.

"Is everything okay? Did something happen out there?"

When she didn't answer right away, Marshall leaned in closer and put his hand on her arm. "Erin, if he—"

"It wasn't anything he did, Marsh." *It was everything he did.* It was clear Marsh didn't believe her. And Erin was definitely not ready to discuss her feelings about Teague with anyone. Not even herself. She blurted out the first thing she could think of. "I overheard a couple of men talking, that's all. It disturbed me at the time, but I'm sure it was just the nature of the surroundings that made it seem nefarious."

"Nefarious?"

Damn. This wasn't exactly something she wanted to discuss either. "I'm being a bit melodramatic. Must be the combination of sleep deprivation and spending time with someone as unusual as Belisaire." Her light laugh sounded hollow even to her ears.

Marshall's look of concern deepened. "What did you think you heard?"

She waved her hand, as if the whole matter was easily brushed aside. "Nothing really. I discussed it with Teague."

"What did he say?"

"That even if I had overheard something—illegal, or potentially illegal—taking place, it wasn't enough evidence to make contacting the police worthwhile."

She looked back at Marshall, but he seemed lost in thought.

"I'm sure he was right," he said after a moment. "After all, he would know all about that."

"What do you mean?"

"Nothing, really. Just that when you live out there, you know things, see things. If there was cause for concern, I'm sure he'd know about it." He moved to the door. "Well, I'd better get back, leave you to your work. If you need anything, just leave a message in the office."

Erin had the strongest sensation that Marshall was purposely evading the issue. Exactly what that issue was, she wasn't entirely sure.

Her gaze slid to her tote bag and the small recorder tucked inside. The one she'd flipped on by instinct the previous night in the woods. Maybe a visit to the sheriff's office *was* in order.

❖———————❖

Teague hooked his hands on the black wrought iron and pulled himself up and over the balcony railing. He silently eased open the French doors and slipped inside Erin's apartment.

He'd been home for less than a year, and coming in the back way was already becoming a habit, he thought with a smile.

He hadn't seen Erin since dropping her off at the college early that morning. Or more precisely, she hadn't seen him. After getting Ruby set up for the midday crowd at the Eight Ball, he'd stopped by the campus lab. Just in time to see Marshall slip inside.

Teague had come on business. But the image of her and Marshall talking, laughing, as colleagues, as friends, took him down like one of Ti Antoine's sucker punches. They would suit each other well, he'd thought, fighting hard to be objective. Marshall was part of Erin's world in a way Teague never would be.

The sudden overwhelming desire to storm into the lab and yank Marshall away by his silk, limited edition, hand-painted tie had sent Teague back to his truck. Back to the bayou.

Now he was in her apartment. Smelling her in the air. The chill air. He stepped silently into the other room, flipping the air off. That was better. Sultry temperatures suited Erin's scent better, he thought, finally allowing his gaze to travel to the narrow wrought-iron bed.

Her long lean form was covered with a sheet. And nothing else. He felt his body stir to life. *Not like you haven't seen what's under there, Comeaux.* But something about the way that white sheet was draped over her waist, contrasting the gentle line of her spine and the soft curve of her hip, made him want to slide in next to her. To run his fingers into her short hair, hold her still while his mouth explored hers, turn her to him so his hands could discover what his eyes already had . . .

He swallowed a groan and moved to her knapsack and tote bag. He'd sunk to many lows, but voyeurism wasn't one of them. At least not when the other party wasn't aware of his presence.

Images of Erin moving on that bed, knowing he was watching her, had him tightening further. And cursing silently.

He lifted her gear and moved to the bathroom, gently closing the door and shoving the floor mat into the gap under it before switching on the light. He caught his reflection in the mirror and immediately looked away. That instinctive move bothered him enough to make him turn back and face himself squarely.

What was he afraid of seeing?

He swore and looked away again as he slid open the tote's zipper. He was just doing his job, if sneaking into an innocent woman's apartment and rifling through her things could be called that. Telling himself he was looking out for her safety didn't wash either. The job dictated he know what, if anything, Erin had recorded of that conversation in the bayou. And that's exactly what he intended to find out.

He found three minitapes in the bottom of her bag; two were carefully marked. Her conversations with several locals filled the first one. The second was marked Personal Observations. His fingers tightened on it. Just what were her personal observations about him? About what they'd done in the bayou?

He slipped the tape in his pocket. He doubted she'd wasted any tape space on him, but she might have mentioned something else about the previous night. He tapped the third unmarked tape on his palm, then tucked it in his pocket also, before continuing his search. She'd said she intended to spend the day transcribing her taped notes and conversations. Where was the conversation with Belisaire? It wasn't in her office. He'd already checked.

Erin had said she filled more than one tape with Belisaire. Had she transcribed them first while the meeting was still fresh in her mind? He had to get his hands on that last tape. Find out just what Erin might have overheard, and, God help them both, recorded.

"Teague?" Her voice was rough with sleep.

He stilled. And went rock hard. Damn, his mind had gone into his shorts and his instincts had gone to hell. In any other situation, he'd be a dead man right now. A dead man with a hard on.

"*Mais yeah, chèr,*" he answered quietly, stifling a disgusted sigh. "It's me."

There was a pause on the other side of the door, then, "You just hanging out in there, or do I need to call paramedics?"

He fought to keep his smile out of his voice. "No blood. But you're welcome to check for yourself."

"I'll take your word for it. You going to be in there long?"

He held his breath. Caught red-handed and he still couldn't get his mind in gear.

"Because if you are, perhaps it would help you to know that the rest of the tapes are locked up in the lab safe on campus."

That did it. He kicked the mat away and opened the door. "And why would that interest me?"

He hadn't expected the stomach clutch on seeing her again. But she was all soft, too soft, for the take-charge woman he knew her to be. And her hair, that angel hair which should have been way too short to be this sexy, was all tousled and finger raked. She was wrapped in a sheet. He gripped the edge of the door to keep from reaching for her.

"Because Sheriff Bodette mentioned you seem to have an interest in what's going on down near Bayou Bruneaux."

"Of course I do, I live there. Care to tell me why you and Frank Bodette were chatting at all?" he asked.

He wanted to wring her slender white neck. He also had an overwhelming desire to run his tongue up that same soft spot. Make her gasp again, the way she had in the woods. Make her stop worrying about overheard conversations and think only about him and what he wanted to do to her . . . with her.

As strategic tactics went, seduction was far from overrated.

Which was precisely why he couldn't do it. Not with her. Not that way. He didn't bother to ask himself why.

"It's not what you think," she said, the certainty in her tone wearing away the last traces of sleep from her voice.

"You have no idea what I think, *ange*."

She took an unconscious step backward.

"He was on my interview list. I wanted to ask him about his interaction with the voodoun culture, determine what types of activity they monitor and why. What he'd actually seen, if anything, of their rituals. I set up an appointment earlier this afternoon. He was very friendly and helpful. You'd be surprised what local law enforcement can contribute to these kinds of studies. Sometimes they have access to knowledge no one else does."

Suspicion tightened the back of Teague's scalp. "How coincidental."

To his surprise, she looked away. Guilt. *Ah, chèr*, he thought, *what have you gone and done.*

She looked back at him. "Okay, so I carefully—very carefully—felt him out on what other activities he monitored down there." She stood straighter, assuming a casually defensive posture. "I'm sorry, but that conversation I heard last night still bothers me. I guess I just can't shove it all aside and pretend it never happened."

"Did you tell him about it?"

"No."

He tried not to sigh out loud in relief. "Then why do you think I care about your tapes?"

"Just something the sheriff said. Since I was taping our conversation, he knew how I worked. He was talking about the various things he keeps an eye on down there and I joked about my recorder possibly coming in handy sometime. I guess I wasn't as offhand as I thought, because he gave me this look."

"Erin—"

"It's okay. I covered it. I'd already pretty much come to the conclusion that you were right and what I'd heard wasn't strong enough to risk Belisaire's trust."

"Well now, that's a comfort."

She made a face. "Don't be snide. I'm not an ingenue in these things. I've dealt with complex tribal politics that would confound you. And in those countries, one wrong step and you could be dinner."

"Don't make the mistake of thinking it's any different here, *ange.*"

"I'm not," she said evenly. "Bodette said that if I ever did think I saw or overheard anything unusual or suspect, that I run it by you if he couldn't be reached. Said you'd know if it was cause for concern or not."

Teague bit down hard on a string of curses. Damn Frank Bodette and damn Teague's own superiors for letting the sheriff know about Teague's role down here. He'd told his boss that letting local law in on this was a mistake. Frank was the only one who knew why Teague had really returned to Bruneaux. And that was one too many.

"Not surprising, *chèr.*" He fought to sound calm,

dismissive. "Local law doesn't have time to patrol everywhere. Frank knows I keep an eye on things down there, that I'm aware of what goes on with Belisaire and her followers, and that the Eight Ball is a natural place for information to get passed around."

"Are you saying you're an informant for him or something?"

"Hardly," he said, not hiding his derision at the idea. "But that doesn't stop him from pumping me every chance he gets. The more he can get from me and other locals, the less he has to dig up himself. Probably thought you'd make a nice link. You tell me things, I tell you. Then he has two sources to pump. He's just doing his job, Erin."

"Which is exactly what I thought at the time."

"At the time?" Teague pushed away from the doorframe and stepped closer to Erin. His back blocked the light, casting her in shadow before him. She didn't back away.

He noticed her grip tighten on the sheet. Just like that he had to struggle to remember what they were talking about. He wanted that sheet gone. Now. And to hell with underworld midnight plots and outwitting an idiot sheriff and keeping a too-smart-for-her-own-good ethnobotanist from getting her pretty derriere in a deadly sling.

He wanted badly to forget all of that and just take her. Have her. Share his need for her. Make her need him in return.

Dangerous. When had she become so dangerous?

"I thought the same thing. Until I got back to my office and found your note."

He grabbed her shoulders before he realized he'd moved. "What note?"

"The one you left in the desk drawer on top of the notes I'd already transcribed."

SEVEN

"And what makes you think it was from me?" Teague asked. "You said you lock up your notes and tapes."

She stared pointedly at the open French doors, then back at his face. "So?" Before he could answer, she added, "And I only locked them in the safe after I found the note."

"And just what did I supposedly warn you about?"

"Not to discuss what I do in the bayou with local law enforcement."

"And why would I warn you about that?"

She glanced away for a second.

"Erin?"

She tightened her jaw. "I don't know. Maybe you have reasons of your own not to want the police all over the place. Because of Belisaire . . . though I have to say from our brief visit she doesn't strike me as someone who needs looking after. And it was you who was so determined to keep me from calling them."

"The only thing I was determined to do, *chèr*, was keep you from ruining your setup with Belisaire by reporting information that would lead nowhere anyway."

Erin's expression softened. "I know this sounds ungrateful. I appreciate what you did in bringing me to Belisaire. But if this note wasn't from you, then who?"

"Who else knows you interviewed Bodette?"

"No one. Not that that means anything. News travels fast. I can think of two other people who wouldn't like me talking to the law." Then just as quickly she shrugged that off. "No. No way did those two men know I was there. And I honestly don't see them coming on campus to warn me."

"You are right about that, *ange*. Followers of Belisaire, if indeed they were, have a number of other very convincing options at their fingertips to scare you away."

He saw her shiver and draw the sheet tighter.

He stepped closer. "That's right, *chèr*. Don't ever underestimate Belisaire's reach."

"I don't."

He studied her face. "Did you record the conversation last night, Erin?"

Her eyes flared briefly with renewed suspicion, then it was gone as she let out a sigh. "Is that why you're here? Protecting Belisaire's people?"

"Like you said, Belisaire rarely needs protecting."

"Then why are you here?"

Teague lightly traced a finger across the soft rise of skin just above the sheet. He was more gratified than he should have been by her soft gasp.

"I told you I'd taste you again. Perhaps I just got hungry, *chèr*." It was the truth. The instant he felt her skin, alive and warm, under his, he knew the job was an excuse to touch her. Not the other way around.

She broke away from his light caress, moving deeper into the shadows. "And maybe I don't appreciate being a convenient midnight snack when your other plans aren't working."

"Trust me, *mon ange*, there is nothing remotely convenient about you."

"Yeah well, so what else is new in the life of Erin McClure."

There was no self-pity in her tone, just acceptance.

"I know all about being an inconvenience, *chèr*." He reached out and ran the side of his thumb along her cheek. "I learned a long time ago not to fight it. To use it."

He felt more than heard her light shuddering breath and closed the distance between them. He pressed his fingertips into her hair and tilted her head back. "I suspect you figured that out long ago too." He lowered his mouth. "Let's be inconvenient together, Erin McClure. I really do need to taste you again, *chèr*."

She opened eyelids that had drifted half shut at his touch and held his gaze. "*Mais yeah*, Teague." Then on a soft exhalation, "*Mais yeah.*"

A groan escaped his throat as his mouth closed over hers. The sensation of being welcomed home stole through him. Too provocative, too much what he needed but didn't want. And yet he couldn't turn away from the danger. She was too perfect, made just for him.

He pulled her into his arms, wrapping her in his body. Yet, when she let go of the sheet to hold him instead, he felt as if he were the one being sheltered, cradled.

Another groan escaped his throat, long, low and guttural. He buried his face in her neck, breathing hard.

"Erin." The word was both plea and demand.

She was kissing his neck, pressing her teeth gently against the vein that pulsed wildly under her mouth. He felt her lips travel to the neckline of his T-shirt, then breathed in sharply when her hands found the warm skin at his waist as she pulled his shirt from his jeans.

"Teague, your skin, you're so hot, *chèr*."

She pushed his shirt over his chest, then lowered her face to the soft hair that swirled between his pectorals. The kiss she pressed there made him shudder. The light trace of her tongue as she moved it up to his neck threatened his control.

He tilted his head back. She took the movement as an invitation. Had it been? He was no longer certain. Nor did he care.

He held her waist in a tight grip, as she ran her tongue up along his throat, then gently closed her teeth around his chin. Her hands were all over him. Tracing his arms, shoulders, down his back, around his waist, slowly up his chest, molding the muscles there.

He'd allowed himself to be touched, but never seduced. Not like this. This was a conscious act of surrender, and yet he had no choice in the matter. Not with her.

As she claimed his mouth again, and he let himself get lost in hers, he discovered a need he'd thought dead and buried.

The need to be loved, cherished. To be needed. In this way. In all ways.

It terrified him.

But the forbidden thrall of it enticed him more. Darkness was all he'd known where love was concerned. Love and need had always led to pain and suffering . . . so he had long ago turned away from them both.

"Teague." His name was a raw whisper of need.

His response was hardly more than a moan. His body felt heavy, languid, a sponge soaking up sensation after heady sensation. He was unable—unwilling—to move, to chance breaking this spell she'd cast over him, more terrified he'd never again feel this way, than of the emotions she was dredging up in him.

"I need you."

His knees actually buckled. His arms came around her in a fierce hug.

She didn't seem to mind, her arms held him just as tightly.

"Please."

He shuddered. "Don't ever beg me, Erin. I'm not—I can't be—" He swore under his breath.

She tilted her head back, forcing him to loosen his hold and look at her.

"I know. But you can be what I need right now," she said quietly. "Is that enough for you?"

He groaned, then kissed her. Long and hard.

No! Never enough, his mind railed. He raised his head. "Yes."

Erin looked into his black eyes and began to shake. She'd thought she understood what she was asking. But now everything had changed. She was sure of nothing.

Because the last thing she expected to see in his voodoo eyes was vulnerability.

And yet, it was also the one thing she couldn't ignore.

Connected. That's how she felt in this moment, as they stared at each other. The impact of that rocked her, should have frightened her.

Instead it gave her strength.

"Yes," she whispered back, finally. "It will be enough." And when he took over the kiss this time, she knew that she lied.

His mouth possessed her in a way that made her feel cherished, needed, owned body and soul. No, this wasn't going to be enough. She wanted all of that for real.

But she'd take this.

He was glorious. She moved his shirt higher, until he stripped it off with an almost violent yank. It made the gentle way in which he took her back into his arms almost heartbreaking.

She pressed her mouth to his stubbled jaw. It felt good, sharp, alive against the softness of her lips.

She buried her nose in his neck, tasting the light

tang of salt while she breathed in the scent of the summer heat on his skin.

She pushed him gently and after a moment he released his tight hold. As slowly as she was able, she looked at him, from the strong legs still encased in weathered jeans, over the flat belly and up to the chest she'd tasted and touched. She studied his hands, the long strong fingers and broad palms, and shivered at the idea of them touching, holding, all of her. Her gaze traveled over muscled forearms and biceps to his broad shoulders, to his neck, then along his jawline. She paused on his mouth. Those wide sensual lips. Another shiver raced over her and she lifted her hands to cup her breasts without even being aware of it.

His low growl jerked her gaze to his eyes.

Black fire. That's what they were now.

"Mon dieu, you are trying to kill me, *ange."*

She trembled to hear his need for her.

"Beautiful," he whispered. He stepped up against her, covering her hands with his own. She gasped, the intensity of the pleasure he took in her actions immediately erasing any embarrassment she might have felt.

When he molded his hands to hers, manipulating her nipples with her own fingers under his, she thought she might explode from the wild, aching pleasure of it.

She moaned, swaying into the joint pressure of their hands.

"Mais yeah, chèr. Just like that. We feel so good on your skin." He spread her fingers, then bent his head and touched the tip of his tongue to one nipple.

A short soft scream escaped her mouth before she bit her bottom lip to keep her mouth shut.

Teague immediately lifted his head, kissed her lips apart.

"No, don't hold back. Release, Erin. Let go. I'll catch you, *ange.*"

She took in several steadying breaths.

"What about you, Teague? Do you ever let go?"

He took a heartbeat too long to cover his surprise.

"You can let go here, *chèr*. With me." She leaned down and ran her tongue over his nipple, making him gasp and shiver at the unexpected act.

His hands gripped her shoulders and she lifted her gaze back to his. "You don't know what you're asking."

A slow smile crossed her face. Again he was unguarded before her.

"Afraid of me, *mon cajin?*"

The fierce light in his eyes was devastating. "Terrified." He took her hands and laid them on his chest. "But go ahead. Scare me, *chèr*." He took a short deep kiss, his tongue pushing hard and fast in her mouth. In and gone, like the thief she'd once accused him of being. "We might just catch each other before this is all over."

His boldly delivered challenge was all it took. Erin kissed him hard, then pushed him backward until he came up hard against the wall by the bathroom door.

So he wanted to play. The idea of playing with Teague Comeaux was tremendously appealing. And arousing.

It was also about the only level of emotional honesty

she could deal with right now. Uninhibited by her nudity—her body was the easiest thing to reveal to him—she wanted only to get him as naked as she was.

She let her hands fall to the waistband of his jeans. His smile broadened.

"*Mais yeah, chèr.* You want I should help you with that?"

She shook her head. "No, I think I can handle it."

He chuckled. "Oh, I'm counting on that, *chèr.*"

She pulled at the snap and kept tugging until the zipper slid down an inch or so. *Oh my.* She swallowed hard. "Dressed in a hurry did we?"

"Something like that."

Between the hot night air slowly filling the room, and the heat coming off his body, Erin felt trapped in a sensual steam bath. She felt the perspiration slide down her throat and between her breasts and lifted a hand to wipe it away.

Teague caught her hand in his. "I have an idea. Come on." He pulled her with him into the bathroom, and flipped off the harsh light, casting them instantly in moonlit shadows.

"What are we doing?"

He turned her into his arms. "I owe you a shower."

"I have bathed, you know."

"Yeah, *ange*, but you haven't bathed with me."

The moan slipped out without warning.

His groan echoed hers. "Oh *chèr*, I do like it when you do that."

"What?"

"Respond to me without thinking." He tugged on

her waist before she could respond. "Come on, let's get wet."

He let her go long enough to turn on the water and draw the curtain. He looked up at her. "Hot or cold?"

"Moderate."

He stood and pulled her against him so swiftly she lost her breath. He stole what was left with a deep, slow kiss. When he had her moaning against his mouth, he lifted his lips from hers. "Nothing in moderation with us, *chèr*."

Erin felt herself sinking deeper into the promise of pure, unadulterated pleasure he offered. "Then hot it is."

Steam filled the room, but her slick skin made her feel erotic, sensual. She watched Teague's skin take on a sexy sheen as he bent to shuck his jeans.

She lifted her hand instinctively, then halted.

He paused, his waistband open and around his hips. "What?"

She shook her head.

"Tell me. No thinking, Erin. Just react."

"Don't take them off yet."

He dropped his hands and straightened. "Okay." Erin had never felt such power, such confidence. She wanted to share it.

She slid open the curtain and stepped into the tub. He caught her elbow to help her maintain her balance.

She turned and crooked her finger. "Come on, come on, *ange*."

Without so much as a heartbeat of a pause, he got in after her, sliding the curtain closed behind him.

"These aren't going to come off easy now," he said.

She slid her hands around his waist. He felt so good she shivered. "Nothing good comes easy," she murmured against the skin below his ear, then nibbled her way down to his shoulder.

He clutched her closer to him, moving his hips against her. "Keep doing that and I wouldn't bet on that right now, *chèr.*"

Erin slid her hands down, pushing at his wet jeans. Her hand hit something hard in the back pocket. It took a second for it to register, but when it did, her hands stilled.

"What's the matter?" he said against her wet hair.

The shower might as well have turned to a sheet of ice. She stiffened and pulled away from him. "I'd appreciate it if you would climb out of the shower. Be careful not to get your back pockets any wetter than they already are if you can help it. I'm not sure if I made copies of those tapes yet."

Not caring if the floor flooded, she yanked open the curtain and clambered out of the tub.

"Erin, wait."

Staying out of his reach, she turned off the shower then grabbed a towel from the rack. Teague took a moment to climb out after her. Even half-wet, his jeans were a hindrance.

She flipped on the light, the unkind brightness a harsh reminder of just how far she'd gone in ignoring her responsibilities.

To the people funding her. To her father.

To herself.

But for once you were doing something just for yourself, the real you, a little voice beckoned. *And it felt damn good.*

The idea that this was all there was to being Erin McClure made her stomach clench. No. She knew better now. But knowing there was more, and that she couldn't have it, didn't exactly improve her mood.

Still, she didn't dare look at Teague. She wasn't any more immune to him angry than she was aroused . . . and she was both. She also knew better than to let him get even a toehold in the confrontation they were about to have.

Wrapping the towel tightly around her, she spied her opened tote bags on the sink. She grabbed them, and stormed out of the bathroom, leaving the door open behind her.

"Just leave the tapes on the towel shelf."

He followed her, heedless of the mess he was making on the floor. He wedged his hand in his back pocket and pulled out the tapes. "Here."

She took them, wiped them on her towel, and dropped them in her bag without looking at them. "Thanks. Please go, now."

He stepped closer. "Thanks. Please. So polite, Erin? To your *voleur?* Your thief?"

"Except for being my guide, you're not 'my' anything. I'd like it if you would go."

He took another step. "You'd like it if we were finishing what we started in the shower." He stopped right in front of her, all big, wet, and aroused.

He was right, damn him.

"What I'd like and what I'm going to do are two

different things. I'm sorry, but being reminded you were here to steal from me sort of killed the mood, you know?" Her breathing was way too fast. She had no doubt he knew just how turned on she still was.

"I had to check the tapes, Erin. I'd have returned them."

"Why? Belisaire? Or because there is something on there that could incriminate you?" The accusation was finally put out between them.

She'd expected him to look angry or guilty. Nothing at all.

But hurt? No. Not once would it have occurred to her she could hurt him.

The resignation that quickly followed tore at her even more deeply. How many times had people not had faith in him? And why?

"I have my reasons, Erin. One was to protect you."

She snorted, her empathy for him quickly dissolving.

He raised his hand to touch her, but when she flinched he dropped it, then looked away. She tightened her grip on her towel to stop herself from doing something stupid. Like reaching for him.

"But you're right, that wasn't my main motivation in coming here tonight." He looked back to her. "There are things going on here you know nothing about, Erin. And I'm not about to enlighten you. For everyone's good. Just do your research and leave the rest of it to me."

"It's none of my business, right?"

"Something like that."

She studied him for a long moment. Just what was really happening in the bayou? And what was his role? She shook off the questions. He was right. "Fine. I don't want to do anything to jeopardize my research either. But there is one thing I want to make clear. I'll trust that you know how to handle things down in Bayou Bruneaux, but the next time you have something you want from me, ask me."

"Be careful what you ask for, Erin."

With no more than a handful of softly spoken words and a look, arousal returned full force.

He moved closer. "Are we done arguing for now?"

For now. Implying they would again. Implying there would be other kinds of activities they would do together again. And again. "I think you'd better go, Teague."

"And I think you think too much."

"Teague—"

"I'll go." But just as she let out a sigh of relief, he closed the distance between them and took her face in his hands. "But you're going to deal with this, Erin. With me. If not tonight, then tomorrow. Or the next night. Or the next morning." He rubbed his thumb over her lips, then pressed it inside. "Taste me again, Erin. I want more." He slid his thumb out and replaced it with his mouth. His kiss was intoxicating. When he lifted his head his breathing was as erratic as hers. She marveled she was still able to stand.

"What are you doing to me, Teague Comeaux?" she whispered.

"Not a fraction of what I want to do, Dr. Erin Mc-Clure."

"But we shouldn't, we aren't—"

He stopped her with another kiss. She groaned and clutched at his arms for support as she returned it with everything she felt, her confusion, her arousal, her need.

When they broke apart this time he released her altogether. She swayed but held her own. He didn't look any steadier than she did. It was little reassurance. Very little.

"Yes, we are." His voice was raw. "And we will. Oh yes, *mon chèr*, we most definitely will."

He walked to the bathroom. She saw him collect his shirt and shoes and ease silently out the French doors. A black panther sliding back into his milieu. The dark, hot night.

"Teague."

He turned at the last second, one hand gripping the doorframe so tightly she saw his bicep muscle jump. He said nothing, simply stared at her.

"Why?"

He held her gaze for what felt like eternity before finally answering. "Because you're good for me, Erin. And I never do what's good for *me*. Just this once, I want to. With you."

Then he was gone, leaving her to deal with the naked truth of his words. And the fact that she felt exactly as he did.

EIGHT

Erin felt the heat the instant she opened the door to her apartment. She stopped the inward motion of the door and rested her head against it. She'd left the air-conditioning on high. So that meant only one thing. Teague was here.

It had been ten days since he slipped off her balcony into the night. She hadn't seen or heard from him since.

Taking in a deep steadying breath—which did absolutely nothing to calm her suddenly racing pulse—she pushed the door open the rest of the way.

Without looking in the bathroom or balcony, she knew instantly he wasn't there. She didn't feel him. Purposely ignoring that unsettling thought, she moved to the window unit. Maybe the thing had finally caved in to the overwhelming forces of nature. But it was humming just fine.

A motion caught her eyes, and for a second her mind was awash in the vivid images of her first night in this apartment. Was he here after all?

She walked to the bathroom door and froze. Dark splotches covered the walls. Even the mirror was splattered. Her gaze swung to the tub, but it was empty. The French doors however, were wide open. Frowning, she closed them, then turned her back and rested against the glass.

Then she looked up, saw what had been left in her sink, and screamed.

Teague took the steps three at a time. It usually took over thirty minutes to drive there from the bar. Erin had called the Eight Ball approximately eighteen minutes before.

Which in his book was still about seventeen minutes too long. Her voice had been so hollow and flat, devoid of all the *vigueur* that was so unique to her. He'd hated hearing her like that. Hated even more the ball of dread that had settled in his stomach.

Actually, the dread he could handle. It was the large mass of fear that went along with it that had thrown him for a major loop.

He rapped once on the door, but didn't wait for her to answer. "Erin?" he called out as he strode into the apartment.

"In here." Her voice echoed from the bathroom.

Calm. To another man, she would sound perfectly normal. All systems under control. But Teague knew better.

He took one step into the bathroom and stopped despite himself. Erin had been rational enough on the phone, but she'd declined to describe exactly what had been left for her.

Teague didn't have to get closer to know exactly what it was.

And exactly what it meant.

"Go on into the other room," he said without looking at her. "I'll take care of this."

"No."

He turned then to find her leaning against the French doors.

"Erin, we can talk about this later, but—"

"But nothing," she said in that maddeningly flat voice. "I didn't call you to come rescue me from the big bad voodoo threat."

"Well excuse me, *chèr*, but that's how I heard it." He didn't say that the fact she had called him for anything had sent a rush through his system that was far too powerful to be good for him.

"I've studied voodoo and seen enough bush tribes to understand the nature of the threat."

"Then why did you call me?"

"Because I don't know enough about this particular following to read it completely." She looked at the *petro gris-gris* desecrating her sink. "I figured you were the one person who could explain this to me."

Suspicion settled like a cold fist around his heart. "And why is that, Erin?"

"You may have been gone for a long time, Teague, but I doubt Belisaire's followers have changed their rituals." She shifted her weight to her other leg, looking for all the world like the weary cynic she should be, but he knew damn well she wasn't. He wanted to yell and argue with her, drag what she was thinking out of her, and refute it for all he was worth.

But even stronger was the urge to close the distance between them and pull her into his arms. To protect her. Which made no sense since she'd made it perfectly clear from day one that she was quite capable of taking care of herself.

He hadn't felt so at a loss since the day Belisaire told him his mother was dead.

"You *can* tell me what this means, can't you?"

"Yes, I can." He opened his mouth, then closed it again. The urge to pull her from the room was almost too strong to ignore.

He'd seen the results of ritual sacrifice before. The ground bones and feathers, the spirit offering of alcohol to the *loa*, or voodoo god being called upon, apparently red wine in this case, the cleansing of blood from the chicken that had been decapitated during the ritual. . . . None of this was new to him. But what bothered him was that it was Erin's walls that had been splattered with fresh sacrificial blood, her privacy that had been violated by practitioners of the darker, violent side of the voudoun religion. This was no idle threat.

His jaw tight, his hands in fists, he said, "Erin, let me take care of this. It has to be done in a . . . certain way. You can question me to your heart's content when I'm finished."

He saw the surprise in her eyes and answered her question before she could ask.

"I'm not an initiate, *ange*. Not like the others. But

I've spent too much time with Belisaire and her people, seen too many things I can't explain or rationalize away to ignore this." He stepped toward her, his control slipping. "Just trust me." He traced a fingertip over her cheekbone. She shivered, triggering a similar reaction deep in his belly. How had he gone a single day without touching her, much less ten?

"Please?" he said quietly.

She let out a shaky sigh. And before his eyes, she seemed to crumble, all her defenses falling in on her. With a low groan he pulled her against his chest.

"Aw, *chèr*." He pressed his lips against her hair, and felt the fine tremors racing through her. "It's okay. Let me take care of this." He tilted her chin up. "I want to."

"I know enough to understand this is more than a mild warning. Someone wants me to butt out. But of what? Belisaire's people? The bayou? My research? I mean, I'm studying plants for God's sake. How is that threatening anyone?"

"You're studying plants and how they are used in voodoun rituals. This is a notoriously closed society, *chèr*. They may not appreciate someone trying to demystify their beliefs."

"But that's not what I'm doing. I don't want to educate them or teach them or change them. I don't even expect them to read my results. I just need their cooperation to do my job. My findings are scientific, hopefully beneficial to the medical community, but it has nothing to do with wanting them to alter their beliefs. Belisaire understands that, or she'd never have agreed to help me." Erin's eyes widened. "You don't think because of the note and me talking to Bodette, that Belisaire would—"

Teague shook his head sharply. "No. This is black magic. This isn't the work of Belisaire or her people."

"Well then, who is warning me? And why? If she approves of me being there, would any of her people do something like this on their own? Or do you think this is related to the note somehow?"

Teague was way ahead of her on that train of thought. He was certain the two were related. He'd spent a large part of the last ten days trying to track down the source of that note. With no luck. But there was no way he could share his suspicions.

"I don't know, Erin. But this wasn't put together by an amateur." He slid his hands down her arms and stepped back. "Until I get this figured out, I think you should pack up and change locations for a while."

Her eyes narrowed. "Until *you* figure this out? Since when did this become your problem?"

"Since you picked up that phone and called me, *ange.*" She moved away from him altogether, and he had to steel himself against the instinct to pull her back into his arms. But her uncustomary vulnerability was gone. The Erin McClure he knew was back. He couldn't escape the wistful thought that he liked both sides of her.

He sighed softly. "I'm the one with the contacts, Erin. I'm your best bet to get to the bottom of this."

The skeptical look she shot him dug in worse than he'd have expected it to.

"I could ask Belisaire myself. I agree, I don't think

she's behind this. If she wanted to warn me, she'd have done it directly."

"Belisaire rarely does the expected, but her way is always direct. I disagree about confronting her with this though. She has other interests to look out for besides her own, or yours." He clearly wasn't convincing her. And the last thing he needed was her poking around the bayou. "Give me a few days to see what I can find out. Then you can do whatever you think is best. Okay?"

"Why do I get the feeling that no matter how I handled this, we'd have ended up at this same point." Before he could comment, she went on. "Three days. Then I talk to Belisaire."

Teague didn't bother to tell her that he was almost 100 percent certain Belisaire knew all about this by now. Of course, Teague was also certain that unless it benefited Belisaire, she wouldn't be budged. But he didn't intend to ask her anything.

"Fine," he said. "Now you go pack while I take care of this."

"Oh, I'm not going anywhere."

"I thought we had this settled."

"No, *you* thought we had this settled." She raised her hand to forestall his response. "I agreed to let you take this . . . thing, out of here. And to let you look into who and why it was put here. But I'm not leaving."

"If this is some stupid female pride thing—"

She laughed. "No, it's a stupid money thing. I have an arrangement here I'm not willing to give up. Mr. Danjour was very generous with the lease. And if things go well and I get additional funding based on my preliminary findings, he's already agreed to extend it at the same rate. I can't leave, Teague. I won't leave."

"You don't have to give up the apartment altogether, just vacate until I give you the all clear." *Until I make sure you aren't in deeper trouble than you can ever imagine.*

"Teague, I can't pay on this place and another one. I'm talking a really skinny shoestring here. Even a few days would eat too much into my budget."

"We'll figure something out." He'd already decided exactly where she was going—to the one place he knew she would be safe—but now was not the time to spring it on her. He could barely come to terms with his decision himself.

"You're not paying a hotel bill for me."

That made him smile. "Now tell me this isn't a pride thing."

"Would you let me if the situation was reversed?"

"It's not, so there's no point in arguing." He had a bad feeling about all of this. He couldn't pinpoint why, but his sixth sense told him it was time to get gone. "Pack, Erin."

"Well, when you ask so nicely, how can I refuse?"

"You want me to do it?"

She shifted around him and walked out of the bathroom, careful not even to glance in the direction of the sink. She was more scared than she'd let on.

Fifteen minutes later, he doused the last of the flames in the sink and carefully disposed of the remaining ashes. He flipped off the light and stepped into the main room, more than a little relieved to find Erin sitting on the bed, tucking the last of her notebooks into her satchel.

"Let's go."

She stood and lifted her gear. "Do we go out the front, or should I toss these over the balcony railing?"

"Very funny." He slid the duffel off her shoulder and walked to the front door. Erin might be spooked, but she didn't let anything slow her down for long. He respected the hell out of that.

She strolled by him and scooped up a backpack she'd left on the chair by the door. "Since you're playing the strong hero here, you can carry this too."

She dumped the backpack in his arms and headed into the hall. Teague stared after her. He was worried about his operation, about Belisaire, and now, about Erin. So why was he standing there grinning like an idiot?

Erin knew she was gawking. "You weren't kidding, were you."

Teague barely glanced at the palatial southern estate as he pulled his truck around the circular drive and parked right in front of the massive white pillared home.

She turned to him as he shut off the ignition. "You grew up here?"

"Almost impossible to believe, I know. Welcome to Beaumarchais, the Sullivans' humble abode."

She was tired, more disturbed than she wanted to admit even to herself, and very confused about her feelings for the man seated next to her, but she found herself smiling at him anyway. "Well, most pool hall owners I know live in slightly more modest digs."

"You know a lot of them do you, *chèr?*"

His quiet teasing went a long way toward soothing her nerves. "Where is Marshall? Did he say he'd meet us here?" Teague had stopped for gas and made a few phone calls after they left Erin's some thirty minutes before.

"Something like that."

Erin's gaze narrowed as the light dawned. "Marshall still lives here. I don't know why, but I always assumed he lived on campus or nearby." She laughed shortly. "Which is ridiculous, I guess."

"You can't imagine anyone giving this up willingly?"

"Not without a good reason." She paused, not sure what to say.

"It's okay, Erin. I'm well aware you probably know my whole sordid story."

"Actually, I know very little. Just enough to know that if anyone had a good reason to make some major life changes, it was you."

Teague held her gaze, and she felt a tremor shoot through her.

"I'm sure you did what was right for you," she said. "And that's the most important thing."

He was silent for several moments. "Thank you."

"For what?"

"Acceptance."

There was a wealth of emotion in that one word.

"Well, I know a little something about that, I guess."

"Yeah, I suppose you do, *ange.*"

And she knew that he truly did understand.

"You're not exactly the conventional type yourself," he added.

"Not so you'd notice."

Teague smiled and Erin felt the heat clear across the cab. "Oh, I notice everything." He covered her hand with his. "And I do like you, Erin McClure. All of what is you." He laughed. "Even the parts that drive me crazy." His gaze shifted to their hands and the way she'd unconsciously woven her fingers with his. He looked back up. "I think it's those parts I like best."

Erin's eyes stung with tears. Ridiculous, since she never cried. But then she'd never been the recipient of such heartfelt words before.

"Don't worry, *chèr*, I don't plan to—"

He began to pull his hand away. Erin held on tight. "No, it's not that. I've just never . . ." She looked down, took a breath, blinked her eyes a few times, then looked back up. His gaze was once again shuttered and she felt as if a cold fist had wrapped around her heart. "Don't do that," she whispered.

"Don't do what, Erin?"

"Shut yourself away." She swallowed. "From me." He tugged his hand once again, but she held on more tightly than ever. "You have your reasons, Teague. I know that. But you don't have to with me. Because I do understand. And what I don't, I want to." She squeezed his big hand in hers. "I enjoyed the years I spent traipsing the globe with a larger-than-life father, but back here, my life made for a sort of fascinating side show attraction. People ogled and questioned, but rarely looked past the exotic trappings to the real person inside. So you're right, I do know what it's like not to be accepted for who and what I am. And it's especially hard when you think who and what you are isn't such a bad deal."

He lowered his gaze to her hand on his, then slowly turned his palm upright and rewove his fingers between hers. "That's just it. I'm probably the worst deal you could make, Erin McClure." Then he tugged her hand and she slid across the seat and into his arms. "Just don't deal me out yet, okay *chèr?*"

"*Mais yeah, ange,*" she whispered back. "The deal is on."

His mouth, when it came down on hers, was warm, wet, and gently persistent. An entirely different kiss than the ones in the bayou, yet far more powerful. Erin was immediately intoxicated.

She opened to him and he took, slowly, thoroughly, until her entire body felt like just-melted candle wax. Pliant, languid, heated.

He lifted his head, his gaze on her face for several long heart-pounding moments. Then she looked at his mouth, those lips, damp from kissing hers, and a small moan escaped her. He groaned deep in his throat and took her mouth again.

This kiss was hard, needy, demanding. She returned it, taking from him as he took from her.

The sound of someone clearing his throat made

Erin jump, her squeal of surprise swallowed by Teague's mouth on hers. Swearing under his breath, Teague gently shifted her from his arms before turning to greet their unannounced company.

Marshall stood on the other side of the truck door, his expression unreadable. Erin struggled to pull herself together. Knowing her cheeks were red and her lips somewhat swollen didn't make it any easier.

"Marsh, I need a favor," Teague said.

"So you said on the phone." If he was surprised by the request, it didn't show. "I assume this has to do with Dr. McClure here."

Erin frowned. Dr. McClure? Marsh had been calling her Erin since practically the day they'd met.

"I want her to stay here, at least for the next few days."

"What?" Erin demanded, butting into the conversation. "I couldn't possibly stay here."

Marsh bent down and looked past Teague to her. "It's no problem. I'll just have Mazzy open up one of the upper level bedrooms. You're welcome to stay as long as you want."

"Thank you," Teague answered for her. He pushed open the door. "Let's get your gear."

"You seem to think this issue is settled." Erin leaned over a bit so she could address both men. "I appreciate the thought and your concern." More quietly, directed to his ears only, she said, "I imagine there is more to this than a simple request. Don't do this for me, Teague."

Before he could protest, she turned her attention to

Marshall. "And I appreciate your willingness to help. I just don't think it would be wise to stay here. Collegiate politics and all that. Me staying here . . . well, this is a small southern town, Marshall."

He shook his head. "The Sullivan name goes a long way toward taking care of all that, Erin. And, believe it or not, helping you in this way will actually score points with the dean. He's counting on you getting that grant extension and bringing more attention to the college."

Teague slid out of the truck and was around back lifting out her gear before she could get her door open.

Marshall met her as she climbed out. "It's none of my business what's going on, but—"

"You mean Teague didn't explain?" It occurred to Erin then that Marshall might be wondering all kinds of things after what he'd just witnessed between her and his half brother.

"He called and asked if he could borrow a room for a week or so."

Erin's eyes widened. "And you didn't ask why? Has he done this before?" She shook her head. "Never mind, I know he hasn't. I appreciate the offer. I'll try not to be in the way. And I doubt I'll be here a full week."

Marshall smiled. "Mazzy loves fussing over company. And with Father out of the country for the next month at least, you'll be lucky to escape before Labor Day."

"Mazzy?"

"Our housekeeper and reigning instiller of terror and decorum." This time his smile was more sincere.

"You handled Belisaire, you and Mazzy'll get along famously, I'm sure."

Knowing there was no tactful retreat at this point, Erin said, "Then thank you, Marshall. I appreciate your generosity."

"Oh, don't thank me. The Sullivans are renowned for their generosity. I'm only following family tradition." His sarcasm was obvious, but he turned to get her gear before Erin could comment on it.

By the time she caught up with him, Teague was saying, "I appreciate this."

"I owe you one anyway." Marshall bent to pick up her duffel. "That's what families are for."

Erin thought she saw Teague wince, but by the time Marshall disappeared into the house, his expression was guarded again.

He turned to her. "I'll be in touch later today. Stay here until you hear from me. If you want to go to your office later, let Marshall take you. Or wait for me."

Erin stared at him. "You're serious, aren't you?"

"Dead."

She swallowed despite herself. "Do you really think we need to go to this extent because someone left a—"

"Erin, promise me you won't leave here without Marshall or until you hear from me."

Retreating, but with full intentions of mounting an attack later from a different front, she nodded. "I brought my notes and tapes. I can work here." She pulled her backpack on. "And I do appreciate this." She glanced at the house. "Hard to bitch about the accommodations."

His expression softened, and Erin felt that pull deep in her belly again. "I'll be in touch, *chèr*."

Marshall reappeared in time to hear the last part. "You aren't coming in?"

He looked at Marsh. "No. I have work to do."

Marshall frowned. "Your first time here in fifteen years and—" He broke off when he saw Erin's eyes widen and Teague swore under his breath. "Mazzy will have my head for dinner and my behind for dessert, Teague," he added, but the light tone was sorely strained.

"Like I said, thank you, Marshall." He walked around the truck to the door.

Erin was close behind him. "Wait a minute!" He climbed in the truck and closed the door before she could stop him. She gripped the open window as he turned the ignition. "Teague, don't. Why didn't you tell me?" He turned to face her. "Why?"

He stared at her for several long moments, then simply said, "Wait for me, okay?"

She sighed in defeat. "I'll try."

He frowned. "Don't try. Do it. Promise me."

"What makes you think my promises are any good?"

He didn't so much as blink. "Promise me."

"Okay, okay, I promise."

He nodded, satisfied. Then he was gone, leaving her standing in the driveway slightly out of breath.

She'd just been given a gift, the magnitude of which she was only beginning to understand.

His trust.

NINE

"I swear, man, I have no idea who did it." Skeeter took another hard pull on the butt squeezed between his thick fingers before tossing it into the bayou.

"Somebody's nervous," Teague said sharply. "You said you'd made it clear to Arnaud's people that she wouldn't be a problem, that I had it under control. If someone from our side did anything to make him suspicious this close to the buy down, heads won't be the only thing that roll."

Skeeter pushed off the side of the boathouse and paced to the end of the pier and back. He shook his head. "No, no. I was with Johnny this afternoon. Arnaud confides totally in him. I tell you, everything is cool."

Teague swore under his breath. Then who the hell was messing with Erin? Could it really be a coincidence? Just one of Belisaire's people upset enough with her intrusion to do something foolish? And what about that first note?

Well, if that was the case, Belisaire would find out and handle it her own way. But Teague had to be certain.

And that meant talking to Belisaire.

Frustrated and more tense than he'd like to be to stay sharp, Teague turned back to Skeeter. "Set up the buy for Sunday like we planned. I don't want anything to spook Arnaud. I've got a meeting later tonight with the Haitian contact. Make sure the boats will be here on time. I'll be in touch." Without waiting for a reply he turned to leave, then stopped and turned back.

"I've busted my ass for almost a year playing two sides against the middle, Skeet. We're this close." He held his fingers up in a pinching motion. "But deal or no deal, I don't want anyone messing with Dr. McClure again. You hear anything, *anything*, you contact me immediately. Hear?"

"*Mais yeah*, Teague. Will do, man."

Teague strode back up the path toward Belisaire's *hounfour*. He sincerely hoped she was unoccupied at the moment. His patience was at an all-time low and, love her though he did, Belisaire tried it at the best of times.

He steadfastly refused to think of Erin and where she was at the moment. He'd done the right thing in putting her there. Beaumarchais was the safest place she could be. If she stayed there.

He frowned as feelings he'd repressed for too many years crept back to haunt him. He'd expected to feel many things upon seeing Beaumarchais again—betrayal, confusion, anger, hatred—but not emptiness. He felt hollow, to the point of a physical ache.

The worst part of it was, until he stood there in the shadow of the home he'd been born in, he hadn't realized he'd been hollow all along. Beaumarchais owned a part of him no matter how fast and far he'd run. How had he not known that?

He'd watched Erin as she spoke with Marshall. She looked good silhouetted by Beaumarchais. As if she belonged. He could visualize her in the large airy rooms, running down the wide curved staircase, sitting at the grand table in the main dining room.

A smile curved his lips. Likely with notes and plant specimens scattered over the cherished antique cherry table, glasses perched on her nose. She'd probably have poor Mazzy growing samples of unpronounceable things on the back sun porch and labeling test tubes for her.

Realizing he'd just had a positive feeling in conjunction with a place that had forever meant only pain, anger, and loss, stopped him in his tracks. He pressed a fist just below his breastbone. That hollow feeling disappeared when he was with her.

That was what she did for him, why he was so captivated by her. She filled him.

"Teague?"

Belisaire's commanding tone snapped him from his startling revelations.

"Right here, Grand-mère," he answered automatically, feeling too off-balance to face her right now, but having no choice.

She moved around the cypress roots crawling along the narrow path and stopped in front of him. "We need to talk."

"Yes, we do," he said, taking the lead, praying she'd let him keep it for once. "Do you know who left *petro gris-gris* in Dr. McClure's bathroom last night?"

"What is happening to Erin isn't the main concern right now, *chèr*," was her only answer.

Teague knew better than to push, but he couldn't resist. "I put Erin at Beaumarchais. With Marshall."

For the first time in his entire life, he'd surprised her, but there was no satisfaction in the accomplishment. Instead it made the hairs on his neck stand on end.

"You did not bring her to me." She studied him closely and he tried not to fidget under the scrutiny. "You are using not only your head in this, *mon chèr*. This pleases me more than you can know." She stepped closer and laid her small, fine-boned hand on his cheek.

Teague looked down into her black eyes and was rocked by the realization that she was an old woman. Though she wore her wrinkles like a tree wore rings—with pride in her strength and longevity—she suddenly looked tired and frail to him.

"Grand-mère," he whispered, feeling a clutch in his chest. He turned his head and pressed a kiss on her palm.

"Yes, Teague, things they change. Soon, nothing will be the same as before. But remember, things that won't show themselves to the head, will to the heart." Her hand tightened for a moment. "And this works both ways, do not forget that."

Without another word, she turned and headed slowly toward her *hounfour.*

Suspicion and dread filled him. "Grand-mère, wait."

"Teague, is that you?"

Teague's head came around sharply. Before he could respond, Erin came into view from a path to his right.

"What are you doing here?" he demanded. "I told you to—" He broke off and closed the distance between them as another thought occurred to him. "Did something else happen, Erin?"

"Belisaire summoned me. She told me you were here and that I was to come."

Teague swore under his breath. "So damn manipulative and to hell with the consequences."

"What's wrong? She didn't say why I was to come, just that you were here and it would all be clear later."

His unease grew. "Oh, she's in fine mystically vague form today. If I could just get my hands on—" He broke off, knowing he wasn't really angry with Belisaire. There were forces at work he knew nothing about, and therefore couldn't control.

"I passed her on the path. She asked that we both come to the *hounfour.*"

"Well, God forbid we keep her waiting." He'd left Louisiana determined to control his life, and he had. Along with everything around it, as well. He'd become cold, clearheaded, thorough, and totally in control of himself and those he dealt with.

Until he returned home. Now he felt as if his life

were spinning beyond his control once again and he hated it. With a passion that frightened him. Because to feel that depth of emotion he had to care. Deeply. Fully.

He didn't want to care. To feel. Not like that. Not ever again.

"Let's get this over with. I have a lot to do today." He pushed past Erin and started up the path. He couldn't hear her behind him, but he knew she was there. He felt her.

"What does she want? You were just talking to her, what did she say?"

"Nothing." And everything. The heart sees what the head cannot. And vice versa. He shook his head, knowing better than to analyze or question it. Belisaire was always right. And the meaning always revealed itself sooner or later. He just wished for once he could see it coming. He had a feeling this one was going to hit him exceptionally hard. "She'll tell us what she wants when she wants. Control is her game."

"Ah, runs in the gene pool I see."

Teague slowed a half step, but didn't look back. "Better than the alternative."

"Yes, but tough when only one of you can control at a time." She caught up with him, placing her hand on his arm.

This time he stopped and looked at her. "I don't want to control her," he said. "Or you. I just want you both to be safe."

"Control the situation that controls us then?"

"Something like that."

Erin lifted her hand to his face. "Thank you."

"For what?"

"Wanting to keep anything bad from happening to me or Belisaire." She smiled. "Although I'm pretty sure I'm the only one that feels that way." He simply stared at her, nonplussed. "I'm not saying I need you to watch out for me, Teague. Or that I even want you to. But that you want to, that you are trying, well . . ."

Her gaze dropped from his almost shyly. Shy? Erin?

He lifted her face to his with a hand under her chin. "It's not just that I want to, Erin," he said quietly. "I can't *not* do it. I—I need to." He stepped closer, his voice dropping to a rough whisper. "Nothing bad can happen to you. Do you understand?"

Erin stared at him.

"I think I do." She cleared her throat. "But if something does happen, Teague, it's not your fault, or responsibility." She blew out a sigh. "That's what Belisaire meant about us making our own choices."

"And what if my choice is to do whatever is necessary to make sure you don't get caught in the middle here?"

"Middle? In the middle of what, Teague? What's going on down here?" *And what is your role in it?* she begged silently.

"You're being threatened. I don't know who or why, and Belisaire isn't talking. I just want to make sure it's safe for you down here."

There was no doubt in her mind that he wasn't telling her everything. Marshall had made a few comments earlier that day as he helped her settle in. They had niggled at her, but at the time she hadn't understood why. "Marshall is concerned about you," she said care-fully.

There was the slightest twitch in his jaw.

"Oh? And why is that?"

"He didn't come right out and say it." She shrugged as if to make light of it, wondering how foolish she was being, intruding where she didn't belong. *So what else is new, McClure? Your whole life is about intruding where you don't belong.*

Yeah, but this time, I don't want to be just an observer, I want to belong, responded that tiny voice inside her. She squashed it.

"He just commented on your lifestyle since you've come home. He sounded kind of concerned about all the time you spend down here. I think he sort of wishes you were more connected with your family."

"I work here. My family *is* here."

"Not all of it, Teague."

"You don't have any idea what you're getting into there, Erin."

"I'd like to," she said, before she lost her nerve. She took a small, shaky breath and added, "I care too, Teague. I don't want anything bad to happen to you either."

He stared at her, his mask slowly slipping away, un-til the ferocity of emotion in his face made her knees weak.

"Then let's go see what Belisaire wants so I can get back to finding out what is going on down here."

"Teague, I want to—"

He pressed a finger to her lips. "Let me do what I

have to do. What I need to do. Then I'll come get you and we'll talk."

"At Beaumarchais?" She knew instantly she'd said the wrong thing.

"No. I have somewhere else in mind."

He was trying, so would she. "Okay."

Teague nodded, then turned up the path. He went several steps then slowed to let her catch up. Without looking, he reached back and took her hand. When she paused, he tugged gently, pulling her to his side.

Erin looked down, heat in her cheeks, a broad smile curving her lips. She darted a sideways glance at him and squeezed his hand at the same time.

Teague didn't drop her hand when they entered the *hounfour*. Though Belisaire didn't so much as glance at them, Erin was certain she'd seen the intimate connection. It didn't bother her in the least. There would be plenty of time later for extended analysis. For now, Belisaire would likely command all her wits.

She didn't have to wait long for confirmation.

"Come, sit." The older woman led them into the peristyle and gestured to a round oak table in one corner of her *bagi*.

As usual, Belisaire didn't waste any time. "We will be conducting a special ceremony this Sunday night. Not public. You are welcome to attend, Erin." Her tone left no doubt that this was a command appearance. Erin didn't mind. She was thrilled, could barely sit still. Finally!

Teague must have sensed it. He squeezed her hand beneath the small pedestal table.

Belisaire shifted her gaze to Teague. His hand froze on Erin's for a moment and she fought a smile. The idea of anyone, even Belisaire, striking so much as a heartbeat of a pause in Teague Comeaux amused her to no end. His sudden tight pressure let her know he'd seen her expression. She barely caught the laughter bubbling up in her throat. For goodness' sake, they were acting like schoolchildren. And in front of Belisaire.

She struggled to compose herself. The ritual. She focused on that. A goal of a lifetime achieved.

"You will come too," Belisaire directed to Teague. "As guide and chaperone to Erin. Answer her questions."

Teague slid his hand from hers and steepled his fingers on the table. He might as well have shouted his discomfort. Erin felt oddly bereft.

"I'm sorry, Grand-mère, but I can't do that."

Erin turned to him, her mouth open in surprise.

"For her to be accepted, you must," Belisaire said simply.

"It's not that I don't want to—"

"Without your chaperonage, I'm afraid I refuse to let Erin attend."

Erin's stunned gaze swung back to Belisaire. "I wouldn't get in the way," she interjected quickly. "Tell me where to stand and I won't move. State the rules, I'll follow them." Erin knew she wasn't swaying her one whit. "I'm honored, Belisaire. This is such an important opportunity for me. You must know that. You have my word I would not intrude. But I do want to be there."

Belisaire's only response was to look at Teague. "You will attend, *chèr*. You must."

The tension in the room was palpable.

"I have other obligations."

"And I say you will be here." She didn't raise her voice, but the order was like a clap of thunder.

"I'm no longer a boy you can command, Belisaire. If I say I cannot be here, you must respect that. But don't penalize Erin, Grand-mère. She has worked hard for this opportunity."

"It will be as I say, Teague. Or it will not be."

Belisaire pushed to a stand, bracing her palms on the table. She stared in silence, first at Teague, then at Erin. Finally she straightened and clasped her hands in front of her.

"You will choose, *chèr*." Her eyes rested on Erin, but she spoke to Teague. "Choose well."

She turned and walked to the door. "I will speak with Erin this afternoon," she said without looking back. "You may come get her in three hours." She left the enclosed courtyard, disappearing into the back of the small house. The echo of a door quietly closing sounded a moment later.

Teague was silent. The tension was still knife-slicing thick. Erin finally blew out a long sigh and leaned back in her chair.

Teague stood. "I have to go. I will be back for you."

So controlled. She wondered if he might explode if she reached out and touched him. Fighting the strong desire to do just that, she stood also. "No. I can find my own way back when we are through. Toutou can take me. I'll call and make sure Marshall can pick me up at the dock."

"Wait for me."

"Teague—"

He circled the table, stopping directly in front of her. "I can't be here Sunday." She saw regret and a great deal of strain. "I would if—"

"This isn't your responsibility, Teague. Yes, I'm disappointed. But I have her attention for the afternoon, which is more than I'd hoped when I came here today. There will be other invitations." *I hope.* Something about Belisaire's tone had been so . . . final.

He held her gaze for another moment. "You'll wait?"

"Yes."

He nodded and started for the door. Erin followed, studying his back as he moved through the house and onto the front porch. What burden was he shouldering? She had no doubt it was a great one.

Without questioning her motives, or her own needs, she caught up to him, slipping her hand in his. His palm was warm, his skin a bit rough. She felt his tension, wanted badly to absorb some of it, relieve him of whatever it was he carried.

They walked across the clearing in silence. Then he slowly tightened his fingers until he gripped her hand hard. Erin felt a sudden burning behind her eyes. He needed to take. She needed to give. Why was that such a hard thing?

She halted, the sudden action half turning him to her.

"Teague." Her voice was a whispered plea. For what, she couldn't put into words. She wove her fingers into his hair, pulling his head down to hers.

His eyes stayed on hers, but he didn't resist. The instant her mouth closed on his, he groaned low and long. His stance relaxed and he turned to her completely, pulling her into his arms.

The kiss was slow, deep. And open to the soul. She felt bare, exposed, yet she pulled him closer. He took her mouth, took her need. But when she was drained to the point of trembling, the balance shifted. And slowly, so slowly it made her throat tighten at the tenderness of it, he gave himself over to her until he too was trembling.

Her breathing was deep and uneven as his mouth slid from hers. She tilted her head back when he trailed his lips across her jaw to just below her ear. He folded her more deeply into his arms. She both felt and heard his sigh when she wrapped her arms around his waist, holding him tightly.

They stood that way for some time.

He pressed a gentle kiss on the pulse point below her ear. "I will disappoint you again, Erin." His voice was a soft rasp against her neck. "I won't want to, *ange*. But I will. And for that I apologize now."

Erin pressed her forehead into his shoulder, his words making her shiver. "Just do what you have to do, Teague. I will too. We'll deal with the rest as it happens." She slowly eased out of his arms. "You'd better go."

"Walk me to the boathouse?"

She nodded.

His hand sliding in hers as they cut down the path was easy and natural. Erin marveled at how such simple contact could be so intimate, so . . . binding.

"How did you get here?" he asked as they neared the pier. His bateau bobbed silently at the end.

"Marshall brought me."

Teague's eyebrows rose. "Marsh?"

"He drove me to the dock at Bayou Bruneaux. Belisaire sent Toutou to guide us in by boat. I'd interviewed him before, so I felt okay about it."

"Marshall came here?"

Erin frowned. "Is that a problem? He didn't want me to go alone. I thought you'd want him to stay with me anyway, so I didn't argue."

"Since when have you worried about what I want you to do?" he asked dryly.

She smiled briefly, then said, "I promised, Teague."

"Did he speak with Belisaire?"

She shook her head. "He saw me to the boathouse. I knew my way from there. I was coming from there when I heard you and Belisaire."

Teague said nothing.

"Is it so unusual? Marsh coming down here? Didn't he come down here as a child?"

"Never. Marshall had nothing to do with my life here."

Erin frowned. "Maybe he's trying to be part of your life now, Teague." She flinched an instant after he did.

"I'm sorry. I don't mean to say painful things, but I don't understand—"

Teague turned and untied the boat. Erin's shoulders slumped. She'd wanted so badly to help, but she only seemed to make things worse.

"I'll be back in three hours," he said, busy with the boat, not looking at her.

"I'll be here."

He stood abruptly and turned to her. "Wait at the *hounfour*."

"Okay," she said automatically, not wanting there to be any further tension between them. "I promise."

His eyes were suddenly so bleak, she couldn't resist reaching up and smoothing the taut skin around his mouth.

"I wish I could help. Whatever it is."

He stood still, allowing her to stroke his skin. "You do help," he said roughly.

"If I understood . . ."

"You'd run hard and fast, *chèr*. Trust me." He pressed a heartbreakingly gentle kiss on her fingertips, then tugged her hand away. "You don't want to know any more about me. Just do your job here, *chèr*. I'll do my best to see that you're left alone to do it."

"That's just it, Teague. I do want to know more about you. Good, bad, I don't care. It's all part of what you are. Who you are." Her voice dropped. "I want to know you."

He jerked his gaze away, uttering a curse under his breath. He looked back at her, then pulled her head to his, kissing her hard, until neither of them could breathe. Still holding her head between his hands, he looked into her eyes, his breath sharp and uneven.

"That's what scares me most, *ange*. I want you to know me. And I'm scared to death once you do, you'll walk out of my life forever."

TEN

Teague pulled the bateau to the dock and quickly tied it off. Three hours. It felt like a lifetime had passed since he'd bared his soul to Erin, then slipped into his boat and left her standing there, her fingers pressed to her soft lips.

It had taken everything in him to leave. He should have arranged an escort back to the *hounfour*, but he'd been so close to the brink, so close to saying things he shouldn't, doing things he couldn't . . .

Swearing none too softly, he pulled himself onto the dock and made his way up the path. He hadn't been able to find out any more about the *gris-gris*, and he was only halfway through clearing his desk at the Eight Ball and getting orders put in when he'd heard from Skeeter. The deal was set for Sunday night. In Bayou Bruneaux. The logistics of pulling this off right in the middle of one of Belisaire's rituals was a migraine waiting to happen.

Arnaud would be there along with the Haitian contacts Teague had been working on for the last eighteen months. But Skeeter had uncovered a tidbit of information that had just raised the stakes tenfold for everyone involved.

Arnaud's boss, the man he acted as buyer for. The man that no one, not Teague, not his superiors, had been able to trace. They didn't have so much as a name or a description. Just the knowledge that he was headquartered in the area. And now it looked as if he might show. The buy down on this deal was apparently too important to trust to a second in command.

If they could nail him . . .

He'd have Haitian and U.S. authorities nailing the suppliers offshore while he and Skeet and their team nailed the agents and the mainland buyer and supplier to points all over the States. A major drug channel into the bayou and the entire country would be shut down.

His bayou. He'd gotten on to this case when they tracked the buyer to Louisiana. When the location hit too close to home, he'd asked to be assigned directly to the case as the middleman. Coming home had been the hardest thing he'd ever done. But Belisaire refused to understand there was danger she couldn't control or contain.

She'd accepted his return with surprisingly few questions, which made Teague suspect she knew more about his true role there than she'd ever let on. All he wanted to do was bring this deal off, make sure she wasn't caught in the net, and slip away again.

But he'd gotten caught in a net he hadn't seen.

Erin McClure.

Sunday night was taking on nightmarish qualities for him. Thank God, at least, she wouldn't be in the bayou that night, since he couldn't accompany her. But try as he might to get his head in the cold, unbiased mode necessary to pull off an operation of this magnitude, he couldn't shake that moment on the dock when she said she wanted to know the man he was.

God, he'd never wanted so badly to be that man. The right man.

But one way or another, his role here would end Sunday. And along with it, his role in Erin's life.

To take any more from her now, no matter how desperately he craved it, would be unfair to her. And, no matter how much he'd like to believe otherwise, to him as well.

Erin was waiting for him on the front porch. Just looking at her made his chest ache. Definitely time to back off.

She grinned when she saw him and hopped down the steps. More time, he thought, I need more time to steel myself against what she does to me.

But there was no more time. She was here, in front of him.

"You'll never believe how great this afternoon turned out to be."

"Tell me about it while we walk to the dock." If his overly abrupt tone bothered her, she didn't let on. She fairly skipped beside him. He'd never seen her so wired.

God, he wanted to touch her. Taste her. Absorb

some of that positive *vigueur* into himself. Infuse his empty soul with her spirit.

"Belisaire let me take samples. Samples, Teague! Do you know what this means?" Her breath was shallow and rapid and he knew if he touched her pulse right now it would be jack rabbit fast.

He curled his fingers into his palms. "I can imagine."

"I have to get back to the lab. Can you take me there? Or I can call Marshall. Or take a cab." Her words tumbled out in a rush. She turned in front of him, walking backward as she talked. "This is more than I'd hoped for. I'll get the second grant for sure."

"Sounds like you'll be busy in the lab for a while. Just make sure Marshall or I know where you are at all times."

Even his autocratic demand didn't dampen her high spirits. "No problem. I'll be working, eating, and sleeping at the lab for at least a week. Probably longer." She twirled away and moved on down the path. "God, I wish Mac was here."

"Mac?" he asked, then scowled at the slip.

She slowed and let him catch up. "My father."

"He'd be proud, I'm sure."

Erin snorted. "Pride has nothing to do with this. He wouldn't care who or how it was done, just that it had and he could be part of it. Which is exactly how I am. Oh, to see his face in the lab." She patted her bulging backpack. "To work with him on this."

Teague slipped his hand in hers. He had to touch her. Be touched by her. "Sounds like you have a lot of respect for him. I imagine he would think the same of you as well."

Eyes shining, she leaned up and bussed him loudly on the cheek. "If he thought about it, maybe." She laughed. "He was always more involved with specimens and research than something as fleeting and insubstantial as people's emotions and feelings. But I understood that. He was an amazing scientist. His ability to focus and let his incredible brain spin out on multiple tangents. He never forgot anything. Incredible man."

"Yes, he must have been," Teague said quietly, thinking that the man's greatest accomplishment was standing before him, totally unaware of how special and rare she was. Totally unaware of just how intensely aware he was of that fact.

"I guess this makes up for Sunday." He groped for conversation, anything to keep him from pulling her into his arms and never letting her go.

"Oh, didn't I tell you?"

Frowning, he pulled her to a halt. "Tell me what?"

"Belisaire granted me permission to attend."

"She what? No, Erin."

His sharp words managed to penetrate her euphoria. "I beg your pardon?"

"I don't want you here on Sunday." In fact, if he could have her out of the state, he'd feel much better.

"Well, you really don't have much to say about this, Teague."

"Erin, we still have no idea who is threatening you. Stepping into the middle of a ritual, especially a private one . . ." A stubborn frown settled on her face and he bit off an oath. "They are generally wild and can easily get out of control. Even Belisaire understands that, which is why I can't believe she'd okay this."

"She asked me to come up early and watch her prepare so I could observe and make notes. She wasn't going to let me stay for the actual ceremony, but we discussed it—"

"Discussed it? Erin, for all we know it's one of her initiates that is feeling threatened by you. Anything could happen." He turned and stalked a few feet away, raking his hand through his hair. Nothing he said was going to dissuade her, he knew that. "Damn Belisaire," he ground out. "She knows about the *petro gris-gris*. I can't believe she'd allow this."

"I'm sure she has her reasons, Teague, but—"

"Oh, I have no doubt about that, *chèr*," he broke in, striding back to where she stood. "But one thing you have to understand about Belisaire, she serves her interests first, her followers second, and everyone else as she sees fit. Don't ever forget that, Erin. God knows it took me long enough to figure it out."

"I can take care of myself, Teague. Believe it or not I've managed just fine on my own in situations far more volatile than this one."

He took her by the shoulders, gripping harder than he should. "You don't know what the hell you're getting into here, Erin. I do!"

"Then tell me, dammit!" she railed back. "I'm an observer, I won't be involved. What are you afraid of?"

He hauled her closer, pushing his face in hers. "I'm afraid you'll get caught up in what's going on and won't see the danger until it's too late. I'm afraid that I won't be there to see it for you." His voice dropped. "I'm afraid I won't be able to stand it if something ever happens to you. I'm afraid I'm falling in love with you and there's nothing I can do to stop it."

She gasped. "Oh, Teague."

"You're killing me, Erin."

She pulled his head closer, then buried her face in his neck, holding him tightly. Against his jaw, she whispered, "Nothing will happen. This is too important to me. I know how to be careful, how not to be seen. I was taught by the best, Teague. You have to trust me."

He held her tightly, his heart warring with his mind. The need to tell her what was really going on in the bayou that night, knowing it was his only hope in keeping her away, was almost undeniable.

She lifted her head and looked into his eyes. "I don't want to cause you more pain, Teague. I don't want to worry you, add to whatever burden it is you carry." She kissed him, the tender pressure of her lips on his shattering his heart. "But don't ask me to stay away. Please."

"Would you?"

She held his gaze. "I think I would do almost anything for you." Then she added, "You're not the only one who's afraid here, Teague."

He kissed her gently. Then it came to him. The one way he might be able to make her understand without compromising his responsibility to his job. "Then do one thing for me."

"What?"

"I want to show you something. I know you want to get to the lab but—"

"I'll go."

He released a breath he hadn't been aware of holding. "Thank you, *ange*."

"I want to understand. If this will help, then the lab can wait."

They were silent as Teague maneuvered the bateau farther up the bayou. Erin's mind was reeling with everything that had happened in the last several hours.

But demanding center stage in her mind was Teague's confession that he was falling in love with her.

It wasn't until he'd uttered the words that she realized how desperately she wanted to hear them. How close they were to the tip of her own tongue. Only his obvious displeasure with the fact had kept her silent.

They rounded a lazy bend and Teague moved the boat toward shore. Erin scanned the gnarled cypress root shoreline for a track or some landmark. Nothing. But one quick glance at Teague—all she dared—showed he obviously knew exactly where they were headed.

He tossed a line over one of the heavier exposed roots and climbed out. Once he had the boat secure, he turned to help her. His hands on her arms and waist made her heart beat faster. Hell, everything about this man made her pulse pound.

"Watch your step. The path is a few feet in."

He held her hand and helped her tiptoe across the exposed roots until they were on the somewhat more stable, marshier ground. She spied the trail. It was wider than the ones leading to the *hounfour*, yet Teague held on to her hand as she followed behind him. The contact with his skin, with his warmth, felt intensely vital to her. Her grip tightened instinctively.

Her body hummed when he very deliberately squeezed back. She had no idea where he was leading her, or where their relationship was headed. But nothing could have deterred her at that moment from finding out.

Several minutes later they came to a small clearing. The swamp was slowly reclaiming the area, but it was still open enough to make out the charred ruins of a tiny house. Only part of the stilt frame and the rear quarter were left, though they, too, were being encroached on by vines and new vegetation.

Teague stopped several yards from where the front steps would have been. Erin watched him without speaking. He was staring at the moldering shell so intently, she wasn't sure he even knew she was standing beside him.

His hand tightened on hers, and after a long moment he turned to face her. She swallowed a gasp at the anguish and pain on his face.

"Teague?"

"I was born here."

Her mouth opened, but she could think of nothing to say. Maybe there was nothing for her to say. It was his need to speak that had brought them here. The dozens of questions teeming in her mind were abruptly dismissed by her need to be there for him, for whatever it was he needed to unburden onto her.

"My mother lived here. Belisaire's people built this for her when she turned twenty-one. She was to be the next *mambo*. All the people treated her as one. This was their tribute to her." He moved forward, stopping near one of the support beams that had held the house above the dangers of the swamp. "She didn't want it. The house or the mantle Belisaire was so damned determined to pass on to her. But she took the house, mostly so she could escape." His short laugh was harsh and totally void of humor. "Not that she could.

"She found work in Bruneaux. Determined to leave the bayou and the stigma of being one of the voodoun behind her. She went to work for my father as a clerk in his law office. Anyone will tell you that my father is not a man controlled by his passions. Quite the opposite. But my mother was different. He was totally captivated by her. Had to have her. His pursuit of her had the whole town in an uproar. Grant Sullivan's image was very important to him, except where my mother was concerned.

"She saw him as her way out of the swamps. His name, his money, his prestige, the respect he commanded, were her ticket to a new life. And to a certain degree, she was right." Teague wandered to the back of the house.

Erin remained silent, knowing he was lost in his past, wanting him to drain whatever was festering inside him.

"But Father's devotion to her was more obsession

than love. He prided himself on his control, yet with her he had none. He couldn't deal with that. He'd be with her, then yell and rant and rave, accusing her of casting spells on him. Hoodoo. Conjo."

"Did she tell you this? I mean, how did you—"

Teague turned to her. "Oh, it was common knowledge." He smiled rather nastily. "*Common* being the operative word there."

Erin almost cringed under the brutality of what behavior she suspected that simple phrase covered.

"When he found out she was pregnant with me, he reportedly went off the deep end. He was convinced she'd plotted it to snare him. And yet he still couldn't keep away."

"And she stayed with him?"

Teague looked at her. "Erin, she would have done anything to get away from here. Away from Belisaire and the voodoun society."

"But Belisaire was her—"

"Mother. Yes, but as I said before, Belisaire's priorities are different from most people's. My mother understood that better than anyone. She was to be the next priestess. It was decided. There was no discussion. So my mother did the only thing she could: she escaped and found a hiding place in the only fortress strong enough to protect her. One built with Sullivan money. But it was an illusion.

"When I was born, she threatened to keep me from him unless he married her. Everyone knew he had a bastard son living in the swamps, the son of a demon woman who'd cast some witchery over him."

"Oh, Teague, surely people on Bruneaux didn't really believe that."

"You'd be surprised. The old ways and beliefs have filtered into much of this area over the generations. People may act like they don't believe, even go so far as to publicly denounce voodoo and all who practice the religion, but let there be the hint of a threat and Belisaire's services suddenly become very popular. Maybe not in person, but there are very few in the parish that haven't sought her out for one reason or another. And therein lies most of her power.

"Even after my father married my mother, which he did only because she threatened to raise his only son in the bayou with Belisaire, the whispers about her never stopped. And others in the parish knew that if the Sullivan name and bankroll couldn't stop the rumors about a Sullivan wife, then it would be social death if word got out of their own connection to Belisaire. No matter how tenuous or well hidden."

Teague dropped her hand and moved away, wandering among the ruins in the front part of the house. Erin followed.

"I can't imagine what your childhood was like, Teague."

"Not easy," he said, an obvious understatement. "I was the proverbial demon seed. And when I figured out that being good wasn't going to change that fact, I decided to live up to my billing. The only regret I have about my behavior was that it made my mother's life even more difficult." He leaned against one of the support beams and folded his arms over his chest. "I used to beg her to leave him, to move us back here. But she wouldn't go near the bayou. This place was literally abandoned the day she married. Belisaire's people considered it sacred. It was hers. No one else would ever occupy it."

"How did it burn?"

Teague looked to the ground.

"I'm sorry," Erin said quickly. "You don't have to—"

"When I was eleven my mother found out Father had been having an affair with a woman in town. Had been in fact since shortly after their marriage."

"Marshall's mother?"

"Yes. Marshall was three years younger than me."

"Oh, Teague. What did she do?"

"Nothing."

Erin stiffened. "What? What do you mean she did nothing?"

Teague smiled, but it was hollow. "She wasn't that strong, Erin. She did what she had to do to ensure her place in Father's life. But the last thing she was going to do was make him choose between her and the woman he'd gone to in order to prove he could have a 'normal' relationship."

"Is that what he told her?"

"Rather bluntly and in front of several of their closest friends."

"She must have been humiliated."

"Possibly."

Erin made a choking sound. "Possibly? Teague—"

"I don't mean to sound callous, *chèr*. But instead of

making her mad, it scared her. She was angry, but mostly at herself for forcing the issue in public. Marie knew better."

Erin swallowed several very unkind words. Then gasped when Teague laughed.

"What?" she asked, perplexed.

"You and Marie are nothing alike, *ange*. You'd fight to the death for something or someone you believed in. You can't know how much I respect that. I loved my mother, I understood her, or at least I tried to. But most of the time she was too busy trying to save herself to worry about much else."

"But she didn't, did she?" Erin asked softly.

"No, *chèr*." He held her gaze for a moment, then pushed away from the beam. "No she didn't." He held out his hand for her.

Erin's eyes burned as she stepped over the rubble and accepted his offer. He led her back to the path at the edge of the clearing, then turned to stare at the ruins.

"Father asked her for a divorce right after I turned twelve. He made no pretense that he planned to marry Marshall's mother, nor did he spare my mother's feelings. Why he hadn't asked before no one knows. For all his anger and adultery, he was still obsessed with her. He dared her to stop him, as if he was trying to prove to both of them that no spell existed, that he was truly free to make his own choices."

"What did she do?"

"She threatened him. But despite her hold on him she was an embarrassment. As was I. Even more so. A true black sheep in every sense of the word. Now he had Marshall. The model child and heir. Blond, handsome, smart. All-American. Untainted by voodoo."

Erin turned to Teague and placed her hand on his chest. He looked at her, his expression hard. But she saw the anguish, the old pain. "I didn't know. How unfair to both of you. You must have despised him, even though he was as innocent in all of it as you were."

"Well, that's the ironic thing in this whole ugly mess." Erin began to lift her hand, but Teague quickly trapped it with his own. She felt the steady pulse of his heart.

"What was?"

"I think I was the only one who truly understood Marshall. Just because his father was a Sullivan and his mother was from a fine family herself didn't remove the stigma of being born a bastard. He was tortured by the other kids as much as I was. Only he didn't fight back."

"And you did." Erin knew instantly how it had been. "You fought for him."

"All the time." Teague forced a smile, but Erin wanted to cry. "He hated me for that. Made it a point never to ask me for anything, never to owe me."

Erin rested her forehead on Teague's shoulder, her heart aching for the boys they'd been. "I bet you didn't make that decision easy on him either."

He pulled her closer. "No. No, I didn't. It took a couple of years, but when Father pressed for the final divorce, that was no longer an issue."

Erin held him more tightly. He returned the embrace, resting his chin on her head. She knew he was staring at the charred remains of his mother's house.

"What happened, Teague?"

"She came back here. The house burned. She died."

His stark summation of what had to be the worst tragedy a child could suffer hit Erin like a physical blow.

"The coroner and the fire investigator both pronounced it a suicide," he went on in the same bleak voice. "Of course the rumors flew thick and vicious, each one wilder than the last. It's been almost twenty years. I still hear them."

"How could she do that to you?"

"She wasn't thinking of me, Erin. Hell, I don't know what was going on in her mind. I spent as little time at Beaumarchais at that point as possible. The day she died I had skipped school and hitched down to a pool hall near the bayou. I spent a lot of time there."

"The Eight Ball?"

He shook his head. "But one very much like it. Actually, I named my place Behind the Eight Ball." He leaned back against a tree and pulled her with him. "Appropriate don't you think?"

"You don't want to know what I think."

He ran a hand down the side of her face and tilted it up to him. She had no doubt he saw the fury in her eyes. "Don't, Erin. It was a long time ago."

"Time doesn't make it right. Or okay." He continued to stare at her, and finally she let out a sigh and let her head drop back to his shoulder. "I also know that all this helped to shape the man you've become."

He stiffened, and she immediately looked up at him.

"Why do you do that?" At his raised eyebrow, she said, "Hide."

His face shuttered immediately.

"See, just like that. I don't even think you're aware of it. That's why I hate what happened to you as a child. I don't blame you for wanting to close yourself off. I don't think I'd risk myself again either. But it doesn't stop me from wishing it were different for you."

"Minor in psychology, Doctor?"

"No. I majored in life," she shot back. "I guess between romping naked with the aborigines and crawling through jungles, deserts, and other slightly nonurban locales, you could say mine was about as far left of normal as you could get. And I guess as a result so am I." She looked away, suddenly feeling awkward and oddly shy. "Maybe I'm not one to preach after all, huh?"

He turned her face back to his, studying her intently. She stared right back, willing herself to relax and let him in. Willing him to do the same.

"Maybe I like exactly what and who you are, Erin McClure. Maybe I do hide. I do know that I don't want to with you. I'm almost compelled not to." He shifted her against him so they both looked at the ruined house. "That's why I brought you here. To lay it all out and explain what happened."

"You didn't have to. Revisiting this . . ." She shook her head.

"You said you wanted to understand me. You were right about the past shaping us. It has everything to do with who I am now." He pulled her back around to him and kissed her hard.

Startled, Erin stiffened for a second, then relaxed fully into his kiss. He groaned deep in his throat and gentled the pressure of his mouth on hers. He lingered, tasting her slowly, so sweetly, her knees went weak.

He lifted his head and looked down at her. "I've never cared what anyone thought of me, *chèr*. But with you . . ."

"Shh, *mon cajun*," she whispered, running a fingertip over his bottom lip. "Kiss me again. I'm not going anywhere."

ELEVEN

Teague hesitated, his heart pounding. A lifetime of subjugating need and want began to dissolve like the surge of the tide eroding a sand fortress. Grains of control, of protective instincts, of anger, of pain, all began to wash away as he stared into Erin's eyes.

"*Mais yeah, chèr*, it's okay," she whispered.

His breath left him as he sank into the kiss she offered so beautifully, so perfectly.

She took his mouth, slipped her arms around him, and held him.

Home.

He squeezed his eyes shut and tried to imprint the sensation of completeness on his soul, to recall whenever he needed it. The hollow ache in his chest began to ease as she deepened the kiss.

He shifted her body so her hips aligned with his. The sweet pressure made him groan as his body hardened against her softness.

"Erin, *ange*," he said against her mouth.

She answered him with a whimper of need that un-raveled what was left of his restraint.

"I need you too, Teague." She pressed kisses along his jaw.

"Oh God, Erin." He pulled her up against him. "Wrap your legs around me."

She pressed her knees to his waist and he slowly slid them down until he was seated at the base of the tree with her in his lap, her legs around him.

He gripped her head in one hand and took her mouth again. And again.

"I want to touch you, taste you," she said.

He groaned. "You will kill me."

She lifted her head and smiled at him, pure joy on her face, fierce desire in her eyes. He felt his heart swell and the bleak spot inside him shattered into a million pieces.

"Then it will be a sweet death, *mon* Cajin." She reached down and tugged his shirt loose. He started to help her. "Let me," she commanded. "I'll let you return the favor. Not that there's anything surprising under there," she added with a self-deprecating laugh.

He lowered his head and pressed a kiss against the beat of her heart, then looked at her. "It's what's under here I want."

Her eyes glistened with sudden tears. "Oh, *chèr*," she whispered. "I think that's been yours for a while now."

"Erin . . . I . . ." Teague paused, his own heart thundering at what she'd just admitted. He wanted to laugh, to shout. Had he ever felt this . . . good? Yes, that's how she made him feel. As if he were good. Worthy.

He kissed her, laughing and groaning at the same time, when she slid her hands under his shirt and ran them up his back.

"If there's a law against feeling this incredible, I don't want to know about it," she said.

He leaned her back, a wicked gleam in his eye. "Paybacks are hell." He slid his hand under the T-shirt she wore.

She sighed. "Feels more like heaven to me."

Her response to him was so perfect. So honest. And just like that, his control snapped.

He growled and yanked his shirt over his head with one hand. He shook it out behind her, then reached for her shirt. She beat him to it.

"Oh, yes." She sighed.

She flipped her shirt behind her, and then he was on top of her, heartbeat to heartbeat. Her knees were pressed to his hips, her own hips arched beneath his.

He nuzzled her neck. "Erin, I want to taste you, I want to—need to—" He broke off with a harsh chuckle. *"Mon dieu,* I just need."

She captured his head in her hands, kissed him. "Then take. I promise I'll cry uncle when I can't stand it anymore."

"You are amazing. I—" He stopped just as the rest of the sentence rushed to the tip of his tongue. *I love you.* The truth of it rocked him hard. How natural it felt to say it. How badly he wanted to tell her. And often.

He was stunned by the ferocity of the need to claim. To possess. To be possessed. It was primal, driving, overwhelming. And he couldn't imagine never feeling this way again. He wanted it now, he wanted it forever.

But she groaned then and arched beneath him. He took the offered pleasure of her hardened nipples and lost himself in her, telling her with his body, his mouth, his hands.

She pushed at his jeans. He made short work of her shorts.

His face was buried in her neck when a shred of sanity crept back into his mind. Panting hard, he managed to say, "God, what am I doing?"

"Making love to me I hope," she answered, just as breathless.

"It shouldn't be here, Erin. It should be—"

"Exactly where we are when it happens." She nudged his cheek and he looked at her. "I want you, Teague. Where isn't important. You are." Her eyes clouded suddenly. "Oh. Wait a minute. Is it because—" she glanced at the charred house, "because we're *here?*"

Teague didn't look away. "It's because you should be on a soft bed. Not on the ground in the swamps."

She giggled.

"What?"

"I've spent most of my life in conditions like this or worse. Far worse." She giggled again. "I finally find a man I want more than I want to breathe, a man as at home in the wild as I am . . . and he wants a bed."

Teague smiled, no longer caring about where the

hell they were, but unable to ignore what she'd revealed. "More than you want to breathe, *ange?*"

"*Mais yeah, chèr.*" She grinned. "Big time *mais yeah.*"

This time he laughed. But they both moaned when he kissed her and slid between her thighs. She wrapped her legs around his waist and he slid an arm beneath her hips.

Just as he pressed against her, she reached up and traced a bead of perspiration from his chest.

"There is one thing we could try next time."

He paused and looked at her, then they both grinned. "Air-conditioning," they said at the same time.

"I'll teach you how to like it hot, *chèr*," he said, then slid into her with one deep thrust.

She arched high beneath him. "Oh, yes," she groaned. "I think there's a lot you could teach me."

Teague felt as if he'd died and gone to heaven. It was the first time he could even understand the concept of heaven. Being inside her was beyond mortal pleasure.

Their bodies established a rhythm beyond his control. He relinquished it willingly. Never before had he just let go. He emptied his mind and abandoned himself body and soul into what he was feeling.

He felt her body grip his, her hands on his skin. He locked his gaze on her eyes as he pulled back on his heels and reached down between them, touching her just above where they were joined. Watching her come apart under his touch dissolved what sanity he possessed.

He bent over her again as she shuddered around him, wild with need, so intent on her and her pleasure he slowed his own body, gritting down hard, pulling back from the edge.

She yanked him back hard. Gripping his hips, she pulled him forward. "More, Teague," she rasped. "For both of us."

He bent over her, completely undone, driving into her, exulting every time she raised up to meet him. He reached the peak, not too sure he'd survive it when he went over the edge. "I don't want to breathe either. Kiss me, Erin. Take my breath away."

She swallowed his moans as he came hard and fast inside her.

Erin held him close, loving the weight of his body pressing hers down. Her body continued to clutch in tiny spasms of pleasure. She was so replete she felt as if she could sleep for days. And at the same time she was so wired she couldn't organize her thoughts.

"Why did you come back?" she asked.

He pressed a long slow kiss on the curve of skin between her neck and shoulder, making her hips roll languidly beneath him.

He groaned. "If you want air-conditioning next time you'd better stop that."

"You started it." She wanted to shout at how good it felt to be in his arms.

He rolled to his side and pulled her around him, tucking their shirts under her hip and shoulder, letting her use his arm as a pillow.

She looked up at him, pushing his hair back.

He dropped a kiss on her lips. Then another one. And another. She moaned and pushed lightly at his chest. "Now who's not stopping?"

He pressed his face into her hair. "What did you ask me, *ange?* I'm sorry I was preoccupied." He nuzzled her.

She arched her neck for him. "Never mind."

He lifted his head. "No, what did you want to know?"

"It's okay, my mind was just spinning and—"

"Just ask me, Erin."

She realized she really did want to know the answer. He was still too much an enigma to her. There was more to him than black sheep pool-hall owner, she'd bet on it. But what that something was she had no idea. Or maybe she did and just hadn't wanted to face it. Until now.

"Why did you come back to Bruneaux? The bayou. After all those years." As soon as the question was out she wondered if she'd just ruined the most perfect moment of her life. But he didn't retreat or shut her out.

That gift alone made her feel so good she didn't care if he answered her or not.

"I didn't plan to."

"I can imagine," she said softly. "Marshall said you left the day you came of age and never looked back."

"Oh, I looked." He broke their gaze for a moment. "I just hated what I saw." He turned back to her. "It was easier to go on than try to fix what was wrong. If I didn't have to deal with it, it didn't exist."

"Ah yes, I'm familiar with that myth."

He traced a finger along her cheekbone. She loved the way he was always touching her, as if he couldn't help it. It gave her permission to do the same.

"Tell me," he said.

"My mother died when I was five. My memories of her are vague, but pleasant. Mac took me with him from that point on. I had lived on four continents by the time I was seven. I had played with children from tribes no one even knew existed. Had helped skin and clean any number of animals and fish in both frigid cold and stifling hot conditions before I was nine. I'd spent nights alone in the outback by the time I was thirteen." She smiled dryly. "To say I was a self-sufficient teen is putting it rather mildly."

Teague marveled at how protective he felt. At the same time he was filled with pride over that very trait she felt so self-conscious of.

"Intimidating were you?"

"The men I wanted to date were put off by me. The ones that asked me out were usually other scientists too distracted by our research to notice that I . . ." The blush that crept into her cheeks charmed Teague to no end.

"Why, Doctor, are you saying you wanted to be desired for your body and not your mind?"

"As a matter of fact, yes."

He rolled her to her back. "Then consider yourself desired."

"A sex object at last," she sighed dramatically, laughing even as he kissed her.

He lifted his mouth and looked down at her. "Is it okay if I desire both?"

Eyes shining, she nodded. "Very much so. Of course, you I just want for your body."

He turned over and pulled her with him. "It's all yours, *chèr*."

She was so comfortable in her nudity, so naturally sexy to him, that Teague began to harden again. He propped his head on his folded arms and just reveled in the joy of staring at her.

"You know we're lying on the ground in the swamp with any number of weird insects and other crawling things," she said, obviously not the least bit concerned.

"I figure since you're a scientist, I'm in the hands of a trained professional. If you're not worried, I'm safe."

Erin smiled. "And what are your hands trained to do besides shoot pool?"

Caught badly off guard, Teague tried hard not to let the reality check show.

Her smile faded. Damn.

"What is it?"

That he could no longer hide from her should have bothered him more than it did. The only thing that bothered him was not being able to tell her the whole story. He wanted it all out on the table now, wanted to deal with her reaction now, before he got in any deeper.

But his personal needs and wants couldn't come before those of his team and superiors. Too much was at stake. Pillow talk was out.

But this wasn't standard postcoital conversation. At least it wasn't to him. This was his life.

"It might be easier to answer your other question," he said finally.

Her brows furrowed, then she said, "Oh, about why you decided to come back to Bruneaux." She balanced her chin on her hands. "It couldn't have been an easy decision."

He shoved his jeans under his head as a makeshift pillow and looped his arms across her back, letting his fingertips draw idle patterns on the smooth skin along her spine.

"No." He chose his words carefully, and hated that he had to. "Probably the toughest one I'd made in a long while."

"So why did you? Belisaire?"

His attention sharpened, but the question seemed innocent enough. "Yes. I kept track of her over the years. I'd heard there was some tension brewing down here. And I knew she would be stubborn enough to ignore it, or think she could handle it. I came back to see for myself, talk to her. We have a pretty turbulent past, but if not for her, I'd be in prison or dead right now. I couldn't just walk away from that."

Erin tilted her head and pressed a kiss in the center of his chest, then smiled at him.

Just like I don't think I'll be able to walk away from you when this is all over.

His throat was tight to the point of choking on words he couldn't say.

"So how did the Eight Ball come into play? Is that what you did when you left here?"

"I played pool a lot. I was pretty good at it. Traveled

all over. Did a bunch of different things." That much was true. "I didn't plan to stay in Bruneaux long, but it didn't work out that way. The Eight Ball, under a different name, was for sale." He looked away for a moment. Everything he was telling her was true, but so far away from the whole truth he still felt as if he was lying to her. He turned back to her. "That was almost a year ago."

He waited for her to question him more closely on what sort of work he'd done, jobs he'd had. He wasn't entirely sure he'd be able to hide the truth from her if she did. He'd used subversion and half-truths as a means to an end so many times it was second nature to him. Protect the mission, protect himself in the process.

With her it wasn't enough. Nothing but everything would ever be enough with her.

"I know how tough it must have been, still is." Her expression became wistful, then she laughed a bit cynically.

"What?"

"Nothing really. I just always used to wish Mac and I had a home. A place to come back to. We had a storage unit. Now I'm realizing that you might not always want what you wish for."

The sweet ache that blossomed in his chest took him by surprise. He had one wish. One he'd never thought to make.

And he had no doubt he wanted this wish to come true.

"Aw, *chèr*. We both survived okay." A slow smile crossed his face. "Better than okay at times."

She smiled, the shadows gone from her eyes.

"Now about your other question." He slid his hands up and cupped her head.

She arched her neck. "About your hands?"

"*Mais yeah, chèr.*" He pulled her head down to his and kissed her. When she was fully pliant against him, he let his hands drift over her back and settle on the curve of her bottom. "Why don't I just show you."

"Mmm, yes." She wiggled on him. "Why don't you."

Erin looked up from the microscope to the clock on the wall above the door. Six-fifty. No matter how immersed she became in her work—and usually it was to the total exclusion of the rest of the world—she had some inner radar where Teague was concerned. For the past three nights, he'd stopped by about seven in the evening to feed and distract her before heading on to the Eight Ball.

Her face heated as she recalled the condom pops he'd brought for "dessert" that first night. By her calculations she'd been safe that first time in the bayou, but neither of them would take risks. She'd forever treasure the stunned look on his face when she casually reached into her desk drawer and tossed that "economy" size box of condoms at him. Good thing her office door had a lock.

And Teague always phoned after shutting down for the night to make sure she planned to stop working long enough to sleep. Then there was the morning phone call . . .

Erin smiled privately. For an independent woman, she sure was enjoying being looked after, she thought to herself, reluctantly turning back to her work. But the smile remained.

She'd pushed all her misgivings and worries about Teague to the back of her mind. One day at a time. One phone call. One meal. One kiss. One . . .

Her work was progressing wonderfully well. She had the ritual to attend the following night—an invitation she was still pinching herself over. And Teague had somehow fit himself right in along with it all. Rather than question the *why* or the *how long*—or the *should she*—she'd decided for once, just to enjoy it.

A rap on the doorframe snatched her attention away from the microscope again. She lifted her head, an expectant welcoming smile on her face. It changed to surprise when Marshall's blond head poked through the open door.

"Hi," she said, pleased to see him. He'd dropped by to check on her, too, had shuttled her things from Beaumarchais to the campus so she could stay in her lab, and generally made her feel as much friend as colleague.

"How's it going?" He stepped into the room.

"Really well. I've got a few more tests to run, but my preliminary theories are holding up so far."

"Good." His smile seemed almost forced.

Erin shoved back her stool and turned to face him. "Everything okay with you?"

He raked his hand through his already rumpled hair. "Yeah, fine. Long day, I guess."

She frowned, not convinced. "Well, you timed it just right. If you hang on a few more minutes, Teague will be here with dinner and he always brings enough to feed an army."

"You two are getting along quite well."

Erin hadn't discussed her relationship with Teague with Marshall or anyone else. She was half-afraid if she had to explain it to someone else, she'd end up analyzing it. Something she'd promised her scientist's mind she wouldn't do.

"Yes," she said simply.

"Is he taking you to the ritual ceremony tomorrow night?"

Honestly surprised, she said, "How did you know about that?"

"Word travels. Will he guide you?"

The awareness that strangers knew her agenda reminded her of the threats she'd received earlier in the week. Since she'd all but sequestered herself in the lab, nothing else had happened. And even though they hadn't been able to pinpoint the source of the threats, the excitement of her research findings had provided a welcome distraction.

Turning her attention back to Marshall, she answered automatically, "No, he has some other obligation that night. He'll take me in to Belisaire's earlier in the day and I'll just stay there."

"Other obligation?"

Erin focused her attention on Marshall. "I don't know what it is."

Marshall looked away, fiddling with several petri dishes lining the table next to him.

"What?"

He turned back to her, opened his mouth, then shut it again.

"Marshall, what is it?"

He hesitated for a second, then shook his head. "Nothing."

"Are you worried about him? About what's going on down there?"

"What's going on down there?" he repeated. "What do you know about that?"

Her mind raced, but she was unable to put the puzzle pieces together. "Nothing really. Just that when I asked Teague why he came back to Bruneaux, he said it was because he was worried about Belisaire. About something she might be involved in or some danger she might be in."

Marshall's attention drifted and she knew he was deep in thought. She'd told herself she wasn't going to pry or ask questions about his and Teague's past no matter the temptation their blooming friendship provided.

But the question begged too hard to be asked. "Marshall, do you know what Teague did when he left here?"

"What did he tell you?" he countered.

"That he played pool. Was something of a shark, I gather. I really didn't question him that closely." Now that she thought about it, she hadn't questioned him at all. He'd distracted her. Her skin warmed at the recollection.

A private smile threatened to curve her lips. He always distracted her everytime she got close. No, that wasn't true. He'd chosen to tell her things she knew he didn't discuss with anyone else. He'd purposely given her very private pieces of himself.

Still . . . She went over the times they'd spent together. When talk turned to what he was doing in the bayou, or the possibility that something might be happening down there that wasn't kosher, he'd answered her vaguely, then diverted her attention.

She rubbed her arms as a sudden chill made the hair on her arms rise. No, there was more between them than that. She did trust him. He'd told her the truth about his past, had been open with her in a way she suspected he'd never been before.

But had that been the whole truth, Erin? a little voice argued.

She turned to Marshall. "Do you know anything about what he did all those years he was gone?"

"Not much." He paused, then heaved a sigh. "Once, about three years ago, I decided to track him down. I guess it bothered me more than I admitted that I had a brother out there somewhere and no contact with him."

"What did you find out?"

"He wasn't easy to trace. He moved around a lot. Mostly the southeastern part of the country." He raked his hand through his hair again. "I finally tracked him to Miami. I know he spent several years there."

"Did you go see him? Contact him?"

He shook his head. "He was working at a pool hall, managing it."

"Didn't you think he'd want to hear from you?"

"That wasn't it. I didn't contact him because he was working there under another name. Had been for some time. I had no idea what he'd gotten himself mixed up in, but I was pretty sure he wouldn't welcome me walking in and lousing up whatever he had going on."

"Going on? You mean you think he was involved in something . . ." she paused, looking for the right word.

"Illegal?" Marshall supplied. "Erin, he was working under an assumed name in one of the most dangerous parts of Miami. What was I supposed to think?"

"Did you tell anyone? Belisaire?"

He shook his head. "No. I'd done what I set out to do. I found him. I let that be enough."

"What about now? Do you think he's in danger? Do you think he's involved in something here?"

An even longer pause this time. "I don't know anything for certain, Erin. But something is going on down in Bayou Bruneaux. I've tried to piece as much together as possible, but it all keeps pointing to one thing."

"What?" she asked, though she knew—and dreaded—what he was about to say. She realized now why she had refused to look too closely at their relationship.

God help her, she suspected the same thing.

"As much as it hurts me even to think it, I suspect Teague, and probably Belisaire, are involved in whatever is going on down there. Right up to their voodoo dolls."

TWELVE

"Marshall—" Erin's mind was swimming. Could the man who had lowered his walls and let her see the most private side of him really be involved in a threat against her?

Marshall slid off his stool, crossed to her, and laid a hand on her shoulder. "I know you're involved with him, Erin. I'm worried about you. That's why I told you this. And to apologize."

"Apologize for what?" she asked, still badly distracted.

"For setting you up with him in the first place. I had my suspicions then." He dropped his hand and moved away, raking his hair again. "Maybe that's partly why I did it. It was the perfect opportunity for us to connect. I guess I was hoping that I'd learn more about him this way. Prove my doubts were unfounded maybe." He turned to face her. "But now you're being threatened."

"The threats," Erin whispered under her breath.

Could Teague really have done that to her? Or had it done? And why?

"When he moved you to Beaumarchais I thought maybe, just maybe . . ." Marshall trailed off. "But now, I'm not so sure."

"What reason would he have to scare me?" she asked, more to herself than to Marshall.

"Maybe you were getting too close."

"We were," she whispered, her heart squeezing painfully.

"I meant maybe you were getting too involved. If he thought you'd get in the way or ruin whatever it is he has going, then it makes sense to get you out of there."

Erin thought she might be sick. This was making too much sense. And yet her heart persisted in finding another reason. "He said something about coming back here to protect Belisaire. That there was some risk she wasn't taking seriously. He came back to help."

"I don't know how she fits in, Erin. Maybe she tracked him down, asked him for help if she found herself in a bind, and now he's involved too. Maybe they've been in contact all along. I don't know.

"I made it clear you'd go into the bayou with or without a guide. That Teague agreed to help me so easily doesn't add up very well."

"He told me all about his past, Marshall. And yours. I know he carries a lot of scars. You must too. He took me to his mother's house. Or what was left of it."

Marshall's head came up fast, his face intent. "He took you to Marie's?"

"Yes. I think he's come to terms with a lot of what

happened back then. Maybe he's trying to rebuild a relationship with you too," she offered, but her voice lacked conviction.

"And maybe guiding you would make it easier to keep track of your whereabouts. To him you are an unknown quantity. And Teague is nothing if not careful." He walked over to her. "I just think you'd be better off back at Beaumarchais. And maybe you'd better stay away from the bayou for a while."

She shook her head. "I'm confused, Marshall. I won't argue that. But I'm not walking away from my work." She fanned a hand to encompass the ongoing research and tests she was running. "I'm finally breaking new ground. Whatever the truth is here, I'm not going to be run off from this."

"Then stay here. Work. But stay away from Belisaire and Teague for a while."

"Why? What are you planning to do?"

Marshall looked away.

Suspicion and dread crept along her skin, making the hair rise. "Marshall? Tell me what you're going to do."

He turned back. His face cold, almost void of emotion. She didn't think someone as seemingly sensitive as Marshall could look so . . . hard.

"I think something is going to happen Sunday night. That things will come to a head that night. I plan to be there too."

"Are you going to confront him? Marshall, if you're right about this—" She broke off as her stomach pitched. Just thinking it made her ill. She swallowed hard. "It could be dangerous."

"Well, what choice do I have, Erin? I can't just sit back and let him do it, let him rip apart this family again." He stepped closer. "And I don't want him to hurt you. Or worse." He laid a hand on her shoulder, squeezing gently.

Erin couldn't think straight. Too many impressions were racing through her mind. She covered Marshall's hand with her own. "I appreciate your concern, Marshall. Really, I do. I'm not used to having people care." She tightened her hold on his hand. "And because of that I'm pretty good at taking care of myself. I'll deal with this."

Marshall crouched down in front of her, his expression open and beseeching. "Help me, Erin. Help me stop him before he does something we'll all regret."

"What? How?"

"You said he was bringing you dinner. Find out where he'll be Sunday night. Maybe I can intercept him. Talk to him." He pulled her hands between his. "I'll be in the building, right down the hall. Just talk to him, Erin. For all our sakes."

"Marsh, I don't know about this."

You have faced the darkness before, Erin McClure. You will face it again. Here.

Belisaire's words from that first morning rang so clearly in her ears she swore the woman was standing right there.

He stood, still holding her hands. "It's your choice, Erin."

The darkness . . . resides in you and one other. Make no mistake, Erin McClure. The choice will be yours. May you both find the light.

Erin shivered.

"You hungry, *ange?*"

Erin jerked her head toward the door. Teague leaned against the frame, a large paper bag in one hand. Her heart pounded so hard she could barely hear him. She looked around her. When had Marshall left? How long had she sat there lost in thought?

"You okay?" He stepped into the room.

It was all she could do not to back away from him, and he was still a good twenty feet away. *Get a grip, Erin*, she told herself almost desperately. She needed time. Lots of it.

The overhead lights cast his shadow across her as he closed the distance between them. She couldn't look away from that dark aura creeping over her, covering her body.

He took her chin in one hand and lifted her face to his. He lowered his mouth to hers and took it. As if it were his.

And in the most brutally honest, unavoidable way, he proved to her it was. Now. A minute from now. A year from now. Forever.

He pulled back and looked into her eyes. His were black. They glittered in a way that made her shiver again. Only this time there was fear entwined with the dark seductive thrill.

And she knew then she was all out of time.

"What's wrong, Erin?" When she stared at him

mutely, he said, "You were a million miles away when I came in, *chèr*." He looked around. "Aren't things going well today? Did you hit a roadblock or something?"

She shamelessly grasped the straw he offered. "It's been a tough one." She pulled as easily from his arms as she could. It only confused her further when doing so left her more empty and alone than she could ever remember feeling.

He stepped behind her and ran a finger along her nape. She loved it when he did that. The shiver was automatic, the pleasure instant and real. *God, what was she going to do?*

"Are you sure that's all it is? I've never seen you this distracted." He chuckled and pressed a kiss to her neck. "At least by work anyway."

She almost leapt away from him. His touch, his scent, the sound of his voice, the heat of him, all of it effectively destroying whatever mental capacity she had left.

"Hungry, I guess." She took as many slow deep breaths as she could without being obvious and moved across the room to the bag he'd left on the table by the door. "I haven't eaten all day." She couldn't eat a bite if her life was at stake; her stomach was a tight ball. But it was something to do. To keep them busy. To keep his hands off her.

She turned with the bag and caught him watching her. And realized that his touch wasn't restricted to his hands.

Could she really feel like this about him and not know him?

Ask him. The voice in her head was sudden and very persistent. *Just ask him.*

She broke eye contact and busied herself emptying the contents of the bag.

Like what, she asked herself. *Oh, by the way, you're not a drug dealer or gunrunner, are you?*

He pulled a stool over to where she stood, and sat down. She tried hard to keep her hands from trembling. "Want me to fix you some?"

"We've got to talk, Erin," he said seriously.

She bit down on her lip to keep the hysterical urge to laugh from escaping. *If you only knew.*

"About tomorrow night."

She stiffened. Oh, God, she wasn't ready for this. She never would be, she realized quickly. Very carefully spooning out portions of crawfish étouffé and gumbo, she fought her warring thoughts. *Ask him. Deceive him. Betray him.*

Her chest ached. Her head was pounding. The steam from the food was making her sick.

No. The idea of betraying him made her sick.

"I know you have your heart set on going to the ritual."

She grabbed on to the one thing she could respond to with complete honesty. "Yes, I do. The headway I'm making on my research is phenomenal, and this opportunity will put me so far ahead of schedule I can get the grant, no questions asked. I don't know when Belisaire will invite me again. I don't want to risk the wait." She didn't even want to consider that there might never be another time. Not for any of them.

"Erin," he began, then paused. He took a deep breath and started again. "I really think you should stay at Beaumarchais tomorrow night."

Erin gave up any pretense of preparing their meal and turned to face him squarely. "Why?"

"Just certain things I've heard. I'd feel better if you weren't down there tomorrow night."

"I'll ask again, Teague. Why?" Her voice was remarkably steady considering how badly her legs were shaking. "What's happening down there? Does it have something to do with the note and the *gris-gris?* With the conversation I overheard?"

"Erin—"

"Does it have something to do with you?" There. She'd said it.

He stared at her for what seemed like a lifetime. She folded her arms across her abdomen, trying to brace the shakes rattling her entire body. But she held his gaze.

A dozen questions were in his eyes. His expression was fierce, but open. "Yes," he finally said.

She blew out a hard breath, sure she'd be sick. She pressed a fist against her stomach. Until that moment she hadn't realized how strongly she still believed in him.

"What's going on down there, Teague?"

"I can't tell you, Erin."

"Can't? Or won't?" Anger was beginning to kick in. It felt good. Too good. She didn't care.

"Can't. Don't you think I would if I could? Erin, there are so many things—" He muttered several curses in Cajun French.

When he turned to her again, his eyes were cold, guarded. That hurt more than anything else. He might as well have slapped her.

"It will all be done tomorrow night. After that—"

"What will be done? What?" She worked to lower her voice. "And what if I don't want to listen after that?" *What if I can't forgive you for whatever it is you've done?* she asked silently.

Or, God help me, what if I do anyway?

It was that possibility that frightened her most. Because even now she couldn't look at him without wanting him. All of him. Body, heart, and soul.

"You aren't going to stay away, are you." It wasn't a question. He sighed, then shook his head. "It's your choice, Erin." He shoved off the stool and headed to the door.

"Just as it's your choice not to tell me the truth," she called after him.

He slammed one hand on the doorframe, then spun on his heel and stalked back across the room.

She didn't move. Couldn't.

When there wasn't but an inch of air between them, he said, "I'm asking for your trust."

"That goes both ways, Teague."

He bit off an oath. "You don't know what you're asking."

"Well, you're asking for a lot too."

The tension and frustration drained out of him in one long breath. It was the first time she'd ever seen him look . . . defeated.

"Mais yeah, ange." There was no mistaking the hurt in his voice, or his eyes. "I guess I was asking for it all."

Teague slipped from the bateau, tying it to an exposed cypress root before making his way silently up the small trail. The pulsing sound of *maman* drums filled the air. He dipped his chin and spoke softly.

"I'm in, Skeet. Out in ten."

"Roger," came the quiet voice in his ear. "Two boats at Marie's. Haitians. I've got Murdock there moving them to the alternate meet site like you requested." There was a pause. "I sure hope they don't get spooked."

"They won't. Too much is at stake. I want to meet Arnaud and his boss alone first."

"I hear you. No sign of them yet. Better make it fast, Teague."

"Trust me, Skeet." Teague signed off, then crouched down off the trail as he neared the clearing just behind the *hounfour. Trust.* The word burned in his gut. He searched the crowd gathered there. The ceremony had just begun.

"Where are you?" he whispered under his breath. He spied her a second later, standing near the house. He took a deep breath but felt no relief. Not yet. Verifying she was there and okay went a long way toward easing the niggling sense that something was horribly wrong with tonight's setup.

He'd been over it and over it, but everything was in place. If all went as planned, it would go down in less than an hour. He'd be tied up for the rest of the night, and possibly longer depending on how things shook down with Arnaud's boss.

He had to see her now. *One last time.*

No. He refused to think that way. He'd been angry and hurt when he left her office the day before. But in time he was able to see her side of it. He couldn't change his responsibilities, and that meant he had to keep his true identity a secret—from everyone—until it was over.

But no matter how long it took him to tie up loose ends, he would come back to her. For her. He'd tell her anything she wanted to know. And she'd listen to what he had to say.

A shadow moved next to Erin. Teague tensed and was almost out of the underbrush when the light of the ceremonial fire highlighted the man's face.

Marshall.

What in the hell was he doing here?

Teague tried to tell himself that Marshall's obvious concern for Erin's welfare and safety was a good thing. He should feel better knowing she was being looked after.

His hands tightened into fists. He'd never been possessive. Possessions had a way of disappearing. Better not to get attached. A creed he'd followed all his life.

But Erin was different. His jaw flexed when Marshall moved closer. She was so damn independent, she'd never be truly owned by anyone. And that was her greatest allure. To possess any part of her was to be possessed in return.

And he'd give everything he was to be hers. Already had in fact.

Shutting out useless frustration and debilitating anger, he focused on her exclusively, studying every inch of her. "One night, Erin. One more night, then I'm coming for you. No more running away. For either of us."

He moved backward until he reached the track, then slipped silently back to the bateau. He lowered his chin and spoke. "Update."

"One boat sighted upriver. Arrival time ten minutes, twelve at the outside."

"Okay. It's party time."

Marshall had been hovering all night. Erin was pleased that he'd accompanied her. Not because she felt the need for a chaperone, but because this way she could keep her eye on him. He'd questioned her at length about her talk with Teague, but she'd finally convinced him she hadn't learned anything.

Nothing she was willing to share.

She'd asked Marshall what he planned to do, but he'd been very closemouthed. Her instincts were clamoring. She had a very bad feeling about tonight. She just wanted it to be over.

One way or another.

Belisaire stepped into the small clearing. Two dozen or more *hounsis* surrounded her. The *cata* and *seconde* drums continued, only now the *hounsis* began to sing and dance.

Her attention was riveted on the scene unfolding before her, and it wasn't until the drums abruptly stopped that she realized Marshall had slipped away.

Her heart pounded like the pulsing rhythm filling the air, as she quickly scanned the area. Nothing.

She had promised Belisaire she would stay near the house. Or go inside if things got out of hand in any way that made her uncomfortable.

The *maman* drums began their thundering pulse. Torn between the unfolding ceremony and a strong sense of unease about Marshall's plans for the night, she finally caved in to the latter and stepped inside the house. Any hopes about him going for a glass of water or something equally innocuous were quickly dashed.

She stepped outside again and did another, more thorough examination of the peristyle. Still nothing. Then she caught a flash of movement, a shadow disappearing down the trail to the rear boathouse.

She followed instinctively, making it to the boathouse in time to see a small *joug* slide from the dock into the dark waters of the bayou.

As quietly as she could, she climbed into a bateau and set out after it.

She couldn't see for sure, but she knew it was Marshall.

Had he learned where Teague was?

It didn't take long for her to realize where they were headed. The direction couldn't be a coincidence. Marie's house.

Erin stayed to the side, as close to the tangled snarl of roots along the banks as she could. She stopped and waited for Marshall to get to the small dock. After several minutes passed, she followed. She was caught off guard by the sight of several small boats and one air boat tied to the now crowded dock.

The thought of the dangers in taking an air boat through the bayou at night made her shiver. Was it Teague's?

She made her way slowly along the trail. The moon was full and bright, but the shadows still dominated the tangled path.

She estimated she still had a few dozen yards to go when she heard voices.

"What in the hell are you doing here?"

Erin's heart began to pound. Teague.

"Surprised to see me?"

"Get out of here, Marshall, before you get us both killed."

"Where's the rest of the party?"

Erin couldn't believe how calm Marshall sounded. Confident. She crept closer, until she could peek into the small clearing in front of the charred remains of the house.

"Marshall, I have no idea why you're here, but do as I say and get out now. I'll answer your questions later."

"You're good at saying that, Teague. Erin wasn't too happy with you the other day."

She stopped breathing for a second.

"I'll deal with Erin later. And you. Leave."

"You really have no idea why I'm here, do you?"

Erin watched Teague's entire body tense as he

stepped from the shadows, the moonlight filtering down to illuminate his face. They were less than ten feet apart now, facing each other.

"Why don't you tell me?" His quiet tone was both threat and challenge.

"Let's just say I have a vested interest in what you are doing here."

"And how is that?"

"You're my brother. I don't want to see you get into any trouble you can't handle."

"And I suppose you know all about trouble, huh, Marshall? You're life is so filled with danger and intrigue."

"You have no idea what my life is or isn't, Teague."

"And neither do you know mine. Now, unless you have something important to tell me, I need you to get the hell out of the way and let me conduct my own business."

"It's your business that concerns me. I think you ought to give some thought to leaving yourself."

On a muttered oath, Teague took another step toward Marshall.

The gun appeared in Marshall's hand so quickly, Erin had to blink twice to make sure she wasn't seeing things.

"Don't make me do something I'll regret, Teague."

Teague froze. "What in the hell is going on here, Marshall?"

"Erin, I want you to step from the bushes and come over here."

She froze.

"Now, Erin."

"Erin, get out of here." Teague's voice was harder, colder than Marshall's.

"She's the one that led me to you."

Erin stepped into the clearing. "Marshall, stop. Someone is going to get hurt."

Teague's attention swung to her. "Did you, Erin?"

She looked at him helplessly. "I don't want you to get hurt." She closed the distance between herself and Marshall. "Marshall just wants to keep you from making a mistake here, Teague. So do I."

"Is that so? What kind of mistake?"

"He thinks you're involved in something . . . illegal."

"And what do you think?"

She shivered despite herself. "I don't know what to think. You wouldn't tell me anything. Then Marshall told me about finding you in Miami, working under an assumed name, mixed up with some pretty rough characters. And I do know you're involved in more than running a pool hall, Teague." She stepped closer.

"Stop," both men ordered her.

She did, but said, "Tell me what I'm supposed to think."

"Why bother?"

Because I love you, she wanted to shout. *Make it all better. Make this all go away.*

Her silence spoke for her.

"I see." He turned back to Marshall. "So what did

you two do? Is Bodette on his way here to catch me in the act?"

"Teague, please—"

He swung to her. "Please what, Erin? I asked you to trust me. To accept what I told you, and what I couldn't. You have a funny way of believing in me."

Marshall interrupted. "We can settle this back at Beaumarchais." He waved the gun. "Come on."

"I'm not going anywhere."

"Teague, don't make this any harder on yourself," Erin implored.

"I'm not going anywhere," he repeated. "You two have no idea what you've stumbled into here. Go home. Call Bodette. By the time he explains it all to you, this will be over. You can have him waiting for me in Bruneaux, I don't care. Just get the hell out of here now."

"Bodette?" Erin echoed. "What does he—"

"No." Marshall almost shouted the word.

Erin turned to him. He was so agitated he was trembling.

"Marshall, why don't you put the gun away. Surely we can work this all out."

Marshall laughed. "So naive. So blind. Both of you. God, if this wasn't so important I'd enjoy the irony of it all." Before she could think to move, he reached out and caught her arm. In the next instant she was trapped in front of him, the long ugly barrel of his gun pressed under her chin.

"Close, Teague. So close."

Teague's stomach turned at the sight before him. It

was beyond anything his worst nightmare could have conjured. Who was this man? And how in the hell would he ever forgive himself if he didn't figure it out in time?

"What's going on here, Marshall?"

"Your mistake, Teague," he said, ignoring the question, "was in giving me something to use as leverage."

He tugged Erin closer to him. Teague used discipline he didn't know he possessed to keep himself from launching across the clearing at his half brother.

"She has nothing to do with whatever is between us, Marsh. Let her go."

Marshall laughed; the sound crawled up Teague's spine. "Why did you have to come back?" His voice was almost a whine. "You almost ruined everything. Almost. Where is your partner, Teague?"

Dread twisted deep in his stomach. No. No way. It couldn't be. "Why did you track me down in Miami?" he asked, knowing he didn't want to hear this answer.

"You're my only brother. I wanted to know where you were. Family ties. Brotherly love." He reeled them off flatly, as if by rote.

"Bull." He nodded toward the gun Marshall held. "You have a funny way of showing brotherly love."

Something in Marshall seemed to snap. His face contorted. Teague was stunned by the hatred in his face.

"You don't know jack about being a brother, or love, or anything else, Teague. The going got tough and you split. Did you ever think you weren't the only one who had it rough?"

"You didn't want my help as I recall."

"No, I didn't. What I wanted was respect." He waved the gun at Teague but quickly pressed it back against Erin. "I was the golden boy. I did everything right. Not like you. I studied hard, worked hard. And I was still Grant Sullivan's bastard son. Just like you. But you gave up. I stuck it out. And I finally learned the secret. The secret to being accepted. To getting what I wanted. I learned that the only thing anyone really respects is power."

"So you got some," he breathed. "How, Marshall?"

"The interesting thing to me was that no one ever suspected," he went on. "I was just the wealthy college professor, happily bucking Sullivan tradition and not giving a hoot." His smile turned nasty. "I didn't want Father's money or prestige handed down to me. I had that just by being his son. By staying. True power doesn't work that way. You have to earn it on your own. I did, Teague. Oh, did I ever."

"Marshall?" Erin's one word was a confused plea.

He didn't even look at her. "Toss me your gun. Both of them. Now."

Erin's attention spun wildly from Marshall back to Teague. Her fear and concern for both men along with the stunning revelations pouring from Marshall made her almost unaware of her own predicament.

"Now, Teague." He pressed the gun so tightly into her throat she couldn't swallow. "I have no problem using this, you know."

Teague tossed his guns.

Erin whimpered, not in fear, but in protest for the destruction that was taking place in front of her.

Any doubt she had about that disappeared with Teague's next question.

"Arnaud works for you, doesn't he?"

THIRTEEN

She didn't have to ask who Arnaud was. Marshall was involved. Drugs. Arms. It didn't matter.

What did was that she still didn't know why Teague was there. But she did know one thing. She loved him. She trusted him. She believed in him.

And she could help him.

She stared at him, willing him to look at her, despite what he now thought of her. That she'd betrayed him, like everyone else in his life, even his own family. She hadn't led Marshall to him, but she had betrayed him in her heart by doubting him.

Erin felt Marshall's body tighten behind hers, as Teague's face twisted in rage and pain. Her heart broke for him even as her mind raced ahead, looking for any opportunity to act. Waiting for the exact right moment. If she was wrong, she could be horribly tragically wrong.

But then nothing about this was going to end without horror or tragedy.

There was a rustling in the trees next to them, and Marshall stilled. "Arnaud?"

A small shadow moved between them, shrouded in a dark cloak.

"Stop!" Marshall ordered.

The cloak dropped.

Belisaire.

"Stop this now." Her words addressed both men, though she looked at neither.

"Belisaire, this doesn't concern you. Leave now." Teague never looked away from Marshall.

"What you do in my swamp concerns me." She turned to face him. "How dare you desecrate this sacred place, Teague. How dare you conduct your illicit business here."

Teague just stood there.

"Belisaire," Erin said, "you don't—"

"I have it under control," Marshall broke in, stopping her words with his gun. "I've stopped him."

The older woman ignored Erin's outburst and Marshall's words.

"I gave you a choice, Teague. I brought her in. I opened the door, gave you an alternative. A way out. And yet you chose to do this instead." She was rigid with fury as she swept the air sharply with her raised hand.

Erin stared at Teague, tears swimming in her eyes. Stop, she wanted to scream. Leave him with something. Someone.

She mentally implored Teague to explain, all the while knowing he wouldn't. And that he should never have had to in the first place.

Shame crawled through her.

Belisaire had asked how he dared. But the real question was how dare they. All of them.

"Move out of the way, Belisaire," Marshall instructed. It was clear Marshall had every intention of making this work to his advantage. As he'd done from the very beginning, Erin now realized. "This will all be over soon. No one will be hurt."

Belisaire whirled to face Marshall.

"You were supposed to help me. To help Teague. I would never have allowed you to attend the ritual tonight if I'd known your true purpose. You told me you were here to help. You will regret this, Marshall." She leveled a finger at Marshall. "You should never have crossed me."

Erin felt the instinctive shiver that raced over the man who held her.

Then, as if seeing Erin for the first time, Belisaire stilled at the sight of the gun pressed tight against Erin's throat. And it seemed as if she aged right before their eyes.

Her shoulders drooped and she suddenly seemed very small and frail. Where only moments before she had been the all-powerful priestess spewing righteous fury, she was now simply an old woman who looked lost and confused.

"Marshall?" she whispered. "What in the world are you doing, *chèr?*"

Marshall laughed, and his hold on Erin relaxed a fraction.

In that instant Erin saw her chance.

She drove her booted heel as hard against his shin as she could. Throwing her head back, she used her skull to smash into Marshall's nose.

"Now!" she screamed over Marshall's howl of rage and pain. She dove for Belisaire, praying Teague would react to her cry.

Erin took Belisaire down in a tumble, trying her best to shelter the woman's fragile body. The first shot cracked over their heads, but their forward motion prevented Erin from seeing if the bullet had found its target.

She felt a heavy thud nearby, and turned her head in time to see Teague roll onto his belly, his gun propped on his forearm, aimed directly at Marshall.

Marshall, blood pouring from his nose, swung his gun to where Erin and Belisaire lay.

"Don't do it. Don't make me do it, Marshall." Teague was panting. "For God's sake."

The gun wavered in Marshall's hand.

"It's over, Marsh. Can't you see that?" His voice broke. "It's already too late."

"Too late," Marshall echoed hollowly. "I guess it has been right from the start, hasn't it." His arm went limp, the gun angling to the ground as he fell to his knees.

Teague lowered his chin and barked, "Now!"

Just then two men in dark clothes appeared from the path behind Erin. Within seconds, Marshall was handcuffed and taken away. A half-dozen other men infiltrated the area, coming out of the surrounding trees like elves.

She saw the pitch on their faces, the weapons strapped to their bodies.

Elves with deadly force.

Teague crossed the clearing, pointedly not watching his half brother being taken away.

Erin helped Belisaire to her feet, neither one of them speaking as they watched the well-choreographed scene being executed before them.

"Are you okay?" he asked.

"Yes." She swallowed hard. "Teague, I—"

"Thank you for your quick thinking." Then he turned to Belisaire, shutting her out. "Grand-mère?"

"Ah, *chèr*." Belisaire's voice trembled, barely covering the short distance between them. She lifted her hand, dropping it again when Teague flinched. "*Mon dieu*, what have I done?"

Teague simply turned and walked away.

Another man came over to them and took Belisaire by the arm, explaining that they needed to question her, even though they knew her involvement was innocent. Belisaire seemed to sink even further into herself. Eventually she nodded, but removed her arm from his grasp to turn back to Erin.

She laid her hand on Erin's cheek. "You made the right choice, *chèr*. Take that with you."

Erin shook her head, feeling her eyes burn and her throat tighten. "We both failed him, Belisaire."

"*Mais yeah.* The very last thing I meant to do." She let the agent lead her away.

Another man approached Erin and introduced himself as Agent Moses Sketowski. Special investigator for United States Customs.

And Teague's partner.

She looked at Teague, who was about ten yards away. After a moment he turned, his gaze pinning her.

"I'm sorry," she said quietly, knowing he heard her. Tears tracked silently down her cheeks. "So sorry. I know it's way too little, way too late, but I have to say it."

When he said nothing and turned away, it was as if a cold wind blew through her.

Her shiver was delayed reaction. The enormity of Teague's role in what had transpired became clear as his partner recounted the apprehension of ten other men, from both sides of the drug cartel. Three men had been shot, one of the drug dealers was dead. All, including Marshall, were in custody.

She stood silently, feeling as if her whole world had just been turned upside down. She wondered if she'd ever get it right again.

And Teague. She looked over at him, deep in conversation with one of the policemen. She couldn't even imagine what he felt at this point.

Once again, he'd been betrayed. By his family. By her.

She couldn't forgive herself for that. She certainly didn't expect him to.

Agent Sketowski touched her arm. "Dr. McClure?"

She blinked once. "Yes?" She felt numb.

"We need you to come with us back into town. We have some questions we'd like you to answer."

"But Teague—"

"Agent Comeaux asked you to come with us. He'll be quite busy for a while. We'll handle this from here on out." He stepped past her and gestured to the path. "Ma'am?"

She looked back at Teague, taking in everything about him, knowing it was likely the last time she'd ever see him.

"Good-bye, *mon* Cajun," she whispered. *I love you.*

Erin pushed open the door to her apartment. She should be elated. She'd just found out her grant was approved. Twelve more months. One whole year. And there was already talk of broadening her area of research, possibly bringing in other scientists with related interests. Their joint study could have a major impact.

"Damn." The apartment was a steam bath. The air conditioner had finally died the week before. Mr. Danjour had fixed it twice, but apparently the problem was irreparable.

She walked over to the air conditioner just to check. Nothing. A movement by the bathroom caught her eye.

She turned, her heart catching in her throat. But the French doors were closed. Her pulse plummeted, along with the rest of her spirits. It had been ten days since she walked out of the bayou and away from Teague.

She'd seen Belisaire twice since then, but despite the

older woman's continued help, she was remarkably, frustratingly, closemouthed about her grandson. And Erin hadn't been too proud to ask. If Belisaire had seen or talked to him, she wasn't saying. Erin knew she should just be thankful she had the woman's continued cooperation. And she was. But . . .

"Another cold shower it is." She stepped into the bathroom and flipped on the light.

"Hello, *chèr*."

Teague was stretched out—fully clothed this time—in her tub.

She had no idea how she remained standing.

He was wearing a snug black T-shirt and well-worn jeans. He was the most beautiful thing she'd ever seen. Her chest ached at the renewed impact of what she'd lost.

"What are you doing here?"

"Hiding out."

"Jealous husband or drug runners?" Her attempt at matching his relaxed humor fell flat. That level of sophistication was simply beyond her. Hundreds of times she'd imagined what she'd say to him if ever given the chance. Now nothing seemed right. Least of all joking.

"Neither." He climbed out of the tub and walked over to her. She trembled, but stayed where she was. She'd withstand anything he had to say if it meant he'd be in her life for at least a few minutes longer.

"I'm hiding from myself."

She frowned. "What do you mean?"

"Actually, I've stopped hiding. That's why I'm here."

"Teague, I don't know what you're talking about."

"Let me ask you something."

"Anything."

"Are you glad I'm here? Do you want me here?"

"Yes," she said softly. "Oh, yes."

Looking down, he blew out a long breath. "Thank God."

More than a little confused, she said, "Teague, listen. I know I hurt you. God, that's not even close to what I did to you." She paused, searching for the right words. "I didn't trust you when I should have. I didn't make the right choice. I listened to my head when I should have listened to my heart."

"I won't lie and say it didn't hurt, Erin. More than I thought it would. More than I thought it should." He took a deep breath. "That's partly why I'm here. I understand, Erin. I know how hard it is to believe in someone else. And how much it hurts when you do and they don't."

She looked away.

"Don't. Look at me."

She did. "I'm so sorry." The ache in her chest threatened to choke the breath from her.

"My first instinct was to walk away. Not to put myself in that position again. I beat myself up pretty badly for allowing it to happen in the first place."

"You shouldn't have had to do that. You had enough to deal with. Oh, Teague—"

"I'll come to terms with my family, Erin. Marshall. And, in time, with Belisaire. I even plan on meeting with my father. I've asked to be reassigned to New Orleans for at least the next two years. Not too close, but not too far either."

Her eyes widened, her mouth dropped open. "Oh, Teague." There was relief and hope in the sounding of his name.

"I won't say what happened didn't throw me, or that I'm not still confused and angry. But with my family—" He swallowed hard on the word. "Maybe it's because my whole life I've thought the worst where they are concerned, but strangely enough, I know that in time, I'll come to some sort of peace with it. At least within myself.

"But I should have been different. I should have believed you."

He looked up at her, his anger and hurt clear in his eyes. "This last week and a half I also realized something else."

"What?"

"I've been running too long, Erin. Hating my past, telling myself I didn't need a home, that I didn't miss the ties of family, of friends. Of people who cared about me."

"And now?"

"I was wrong about the bond of family."

"How can you say that after—"

"Shh." He reached out and traced a finger across her cheek. She shuddered, not expecting to feel his touch. But she didn't look away.

"I walked out ten years ago. I have no idea what kind of relationship I would have had with them. But I do know I have to participate. Without working at it, I'll get nothing."

"Teague, just because you weren't here—" She stopped, then said, "You didn't deserve what happened."

"It'll take time, Erin. It may never be right. But I've realized that what I need goes beyond blood ties. It's about feeling connected. Even if it's disappointing. Even if it's painful." He let his hand drop. "I was wrong about needing a home."

Tears tracked unheeded down her cheeks. "I wish it had turned out differently for you. For all of you."

"Shh," he whispered. "No, *chèr*. You don't understand."

"What?"

"I'm not talking about Beaumarchais. Or even Bruneaux. Or even my family. Belisaire will always be a part of my heart. The rest I'll figure out in time. But there is something special for me here. Something that binds me in a way that has nothing to do with place, birthrights, or blood."

She looked away, but he gripped her chin and turned her face back to his. "You."

She gasped softly.

"You are my home, Erin. I think of you and I feel . . . connected. Stronger. Whole in a way I've never felt before. For the first time I have a purpose. The place doesn't matter. You give that to me." He pressed her hand to his chest. "Here. With me. Always." He pulled her into his arms. "I need that. I need you." He grazed her lips with his. "I love you, Erin."

Teague waited. He'd never wanted anything so badly. Anyone.

"I'm so tired of running. Can I come home, *ange?*" he asked, his voice breaking.

In answer her arms went swiftly, tightly around him, her mouth fused with his so completely his breath became hers. When she finally lifted her head, her smile was so bright he felt as if he'd just stepped into the sun.

"Always, Teague. To me. With me." She sniffed, then laughed and kissed him again. He could taste her joy. Savored it, reveled in it.

"Thank you," she whispered against his mouth.

Relief was a sweet drug that immediately intoxicated him. Pure blinding joy filled him until he thought he couldn't contain such pleasure. He ran slow kisses along her jaw. "For what?"

"I've never had a home either."

He stilled, then lifted his head and looked at her intently. "You do now."

"*Mais yeah, chèr.*" He kissed her hard and long. On a soft gasp she added, "Oh, *mais yeah*," then kissed him again.

"Let's get out of here so I can tell you I love you again."

Her breath caught at his wide, sexy grin. He was her Cajun bad boy once again, but fully open, the shadows haunting his eyes gone.

"More intimately," he added.

She laughed. "What's wrong with right here?"

He looked at her. "I promised you air-conditioning."

"Oh, God," she groaned. "I'm yours for life."

He pulled her into his arms again and kissed her soundly. "You will be if I have anything to say about it."

"Then say no more."

"But there is one thing I need to hear." He pressed a kiss to her jaw, then gently bit her chin. "Badly, *chèr*." He lifted his head and looked into her eyes. "Tell me."

"I love you, Teague."

He groaned.

"What's wrong?"

"That was way better than I thought it was going to be."

"Well I plan to say it often, so get used to it."

"Then you'd better get used to being naked and under me in some unusual and not always convenient places." He tugged her blouse from her shorts.

She yanked his T-shirt from his waistband. "Air-conditioning is highly overrated." She lifted her arms so he could take her shirt off.

He dragged his off next, then groaned when she undid the snap and zipper of his jeans. He nuzzled her neck, pulling her hips hard to his.

"There is one thing I'm dying to know, though, *ange*," he said, his breathing deeper, harsher. "It's been driving me crazy since the night we met."

She shifted so he could slide her shorts over her hips. "And what is that?" she panted against his chest.

He stilled her motions.

She frowned. "What is it, Teague?"

"Just what did happen in Nairobi when you were eighteen?"

She slowly smiled and twined a strand of his hair around a slender finger. "If I tell you, can I be on top this time?"

He laughed. *"Dieu,* you can have whatever you want, *chèr."*

She leaned over and whispered in his ear.

He sighed low and long. Then pushed her up against the bathroom wall.

"You'll owe me for this one," she scolded, not in the least concerned.

"Mais yeah, chèr, but I have the rest of my life to pay you back."

And he did. Slowly. With a great deal of interest.

THE EDITORS' CORNER

Fall is just around the corner, but there's one way you can avoid the chill in the air. Cuddle up with the LOVESWEPT novels coming your way next month. These heart-melting tales of romance are guaranteed to keep you warm with the heat of passion.

Longtime LOVESWEPT favorite Peggy Webb returns with a richly emotional tale of forbidden desire in **INDISCREET**, LOVESWEPT #802. Bolton Gray Wolf appears every inch a savage when he arrives to interview Virginia Haven, but the moment she rides up on a white Arabian stallion, challenge glittering in her eyes, he knows he will make her his! Even as his gaze leaves her breathless, Virginia vows he'll never tame her; but once they touch, she has no choice but to surrender. Peggy Webb offers a spectacular glimpse into the astonishing mysteries of love in a tale of fiery magic and unexpected miracles.

Marcia Evanick delivers her award-winning blend of love and laughter in **SECOND-TIME LUCKY**, LOVESWEPT #803. Luke Callahan arrives without warning to claim a place in Dayna's life, but he reminds her too much of the heartbreak she'd endured during her marriage to his brother! Luke wants to help raise her sons, but even more, he wants the woman he's secretly loved for years. Dared by his touch, drawn by his warmth to open her heart, Dayna feels her secret hopes grow strong. In a novel that explores the soul-deep hunger of longing and loneliness, Marcia Evanick weaves a wonderful tapestry of emotion and humor, dark secrets and tender joys.

A love too long denied finds a second chance in **DESTINY STRIKES TWICE**, LOVESWEPT #804, by Maris Soule. Effie Sanders returns to the lake to pack up her grandmother's house and the memory of summers spent tagging along with her sister Bernadette . . . and Parker Morgan. With his blue eyes and lean, tanned muscles, Parker had always been out of Effie's reach, had never noticed her in the shadow of her glamorous sister. Never—until an older, overworked Parker comes to his family's cottage to learn to relax and finds the irrepressible girl he once knew has grown up to become a curvy, alluring woman. And suddenly he is anything but relaxed. Maris Soule has created a story that ignites with fiery desire and ripples with tender emotion.

And finally, Faye Hughes gives the green light to scandal in **LICENSED TO SIN**, LOVESWEPT #805. In a voice so sensual it makes her toes curl, Nick Valdez invites Jane Steele to confess her secrets, making her fear that her cover has been blown! But she knows she's safe when the handsome gambler then suggests they join forces to investigate rigged games at a riverboat casino. She agrees to his scheme, knowing that sharing close quarters with Nick will be risky temptation. In this blend of steamy romance and fast-paced adventure, Faye Hughes reveals the tantalizing pleasures of playing dangerous games and betting it all on the roll of the dice.

Happy reading!

With warmest wishes,

Beth de Guzman

Shauna Summers

Beth de Guzman
Senior Editor

Shauna Summers
Editor

P.S. Watch for these Bantam women's fiction titles coming in September. With her mesmerizing voice and spellbinding touch of contemporary romantic suspense, Kay Hooper wowed readers and reviewers alike with her Bantam hardcover debut, **AMANDA**—and it's soon coming your way in paperback. Nationally bestselling author Patricia Potter shows her flair for humor and warm emotion in **THE MARSHAL AND THE HEIRESS**; this one has a western lawman lassoing the bad guys all the way in Scotland! From Adrienne deWolfe, the author *Ro-*

mantic Times hailed as "an exciting new talent," comes **TEXAS LOVER,** the enthralling tale of a Texas Ranger, a beautiful Yankee woman, and a houseful of orphans. Be sure to see next month's LOVESWEPTs for a preview of these exceptional novels. And immediately following this page, preview the Bantam women's fiction titles on sale *now*!

No one could tame him. Except a woman
in love.

From the electrifying talent of
Susan Krinard
author of *Star-Crossed* and *Prince of Wolves*
comes a breathtaking, magical new
romance
PRINCE OF
SHADOWS

"Susan Krinard has set the standard for
today's fantasy romance."—*Affaire de Coeur*

*Scarred by a tragic accident, Alexandra Warrington has
come back to the Minnesota woods looking for refuge and a
chance to carry on her passionate study of wolves. But her
peace is shattered when she awakes one morning to find a
total stranger in her bed. Magnificently muscled and perfectly naked, he exudes a wildness that frightens her and a
haunting fear that touches her. Yet Alex doesn't realize
that this handsome savage is a creature out of myth, a wolf
transformed into a man. And when the town condemns
him for a terrible crime, all she knows is that she is dan-
gerously close to loving him and perilously committed to
saving him . . . no matter what the cost.*

The wolf was on his feet again, standing by the door.
She forgot her resolve not to stare. Magnificent was
the only word for him, even as shaky as he was. He

lifted one paw and scraped it against the door, turning to look at her in a way that couldn't be misunderstood.

He wanted out. Alex felt a sudden, inexplicable panic. He wasn't ready. Only moments before she'd been debating what to do with him, and now her decision was being forced.

Once she opened that door he'd be gone, obeying instincts older and more powerful than the ephemeral trust he'd given her on the edge of death. In his weakened state, once back in the woods he'd search out the easiest prey he could find.

Livestock. Man's possessions, lethally guarded by guns and poison.

Alex backed away, toward the hall closet, where she kept her seldom-used dart gun. In Canada she and her fellow researchers had used guns like it to capture wolves for collaring and transfer to new homes in the northern United States. She hadn't expected to need it here.

Now she didn't have any choice. Shadow leaned against the wall patiently as she retrieved the gun and loaded it out of his sight. She tucked it into the loose waistband of her jeans, at the small of her back, and started toward the door.

Shadow wagged his tail. Only once, and slowly, but the simple gesture cut her to the heart. It was as if he saw her as another wolf. As if he recognized what she'd tried to do for him. She edged to the opposite side of the door and opened it.

Biting air swirled into the warmth of the cabin. Shadow stepped out, lifting his muzzle to the sky, breathing in a thousand subtle scents Alex couldn't begin to imagine.

She followed him and sat at the edge of the porch

as he walked stiffly into the clearing. "What are you?" she murmured. "Were you captive once? Were you cut off from your own kind?"

He heard her, pausing in his business and pricking his ears. Golden eyes held answers she couldn't interpret with mere human senses.

"I know what you aren't, Shadow. You aren't meant to be anyone's pet. Or something to be kept in a cage and stared at. I wish to God I could let you go."

The wolf whuffed softly. He looked toward the forest, and Alex stiffened, reaching for the dart gun. But he turned back and came to her again, lifted his paw and set it very deliberately on her knee.

Needing her. Trusting her. Accepting. His huge paw felt warm and familiar, like a friend's touch.

Once she'd loved being touched. By her mother, by her grandparents—by Peter. She'd fought so hard to get over that need, that weakness.

Alex raised her hand and felt it tremble. She let her fingers brush the wolf's thick ruff, stroke down along his massive shoulder. Shadow sighed and closed his eyes to slits of contentment.

Oh, God. In a minute she'd be flinging her arms around his great shaggy neck. *Wrong, wrong.* He was a wolf, not a pet dog. She withdrew her hands and clasped them in her lap.

He nudged her hand. His eyes, amber and intelligent, regarded her without deception. Like no human eyes in the world.

"I won't let them kill you, Shadow," she said hoarsely. "No matter what you are, or what happens. I'll help you. I promise." She closed her eyes. "I've made promises I wasn't able to keep, but not this time. Not this time."

Promises. One to a strange, lost boy weeping over the bodies of two murdered wolves. A boy who, like the first Shadow, she'd never found again.

And another promise to her mother, who had died to save her.

The ghost of one had returned to her at last.

The wolf whined and patted her knee, his claws snagging on her jeans. A gentle snow began to fall, thick wet flakes that kissed Alex's cheeks with the sweetness of a lover. She turned her face up to the sky's caress. Shadow leaned against her heavily, his black pelt dusted with snowflakes.

If only I could go back, she thought. Back to the time when happiness had been such a simple thing, when a wolf could be a friend and fairy tales were real. She sank her fingers deeper into Shadow's fur.

If only—you were human. A man as loyal, as protective, as fundamentally honest as a wolf with its own. A man who could never exist in the real world. A fairy-tale hero, a prince ensorcelled.

She allowed herself a bitter smile. The exact opposite of Peter, in fact.

And you think you'd deserve such a man, if he did exist?

She killed that line of thought before it could take hold, forcing her fingers to unclench from Shadow's fur. "What am I going to do, Shadow?" she said.

The wolf set his forepaws on the porch and heaved his body up, struggling to lift himself to the low platform. Alex watched his efforts with a last grasp at objectivity.

Now. Dart him now, and there will still be time to contact the ADC. She clawed at the dart gun and pulled it from her waistband.

But Shadow looked up at her in that precise moment, and she was lost. "I can't," she whispered. She let her arm go slack. The dart gun fell from her nerveless fingers, landing in the snow. She stared at it blindly.

Teeth that could rend and tear so efficiently closed with utmost gentleness around her empty hand. Shadow tugged until she had no choice but to look at him again.

She knew what he wanted. She hesitated only a moment before opening the door. Shadow padded into the cabin and found the place she had made for him by the stove, stretching out full-length on the old braided rug, chin on paws.

"You've made it easy for me, haven't you?" she asked him, closing the door behind her. "You're trapped, and I can keep you here until . . . until I can figure out what to do with you."

The wolf gazed at her so steadily that she was almost certain that he'd known exactly what he was doing. She wanted to go to him and huddle close, feel the warmth of his great body and the sumptuous texture of his fur. But she had risked too much already. In the morning she'd have to reach a decision about him, and she knew how this would end—how it must end—sooner or later.

Shadow would be gone, and she'd be alone.

Feeling decades older than her twenty-seven years, Alex took her journal from the kitchen and retreated into the darkness of her bedroom. She paused at the door, her hand on the knob, and closed it with firm and deliberate pressure.

She stripped off her clothes and hung them neatly in the tiny closet, retrieving a clean pair of long underwear. The journal lay open on the old wooden bed table, waiting for the night's final entry.

It's ironic, Mother. I thought I'd become strong. Objective. I can't even succeed in this.

Her flannel bedsheets were cold; she drew the blankets up high around her chin, an old childhood habit she'd never shaken. Once it had made her feel safe, as if her mother's own hands had tucked her in. Now it only made her remember how false a comfort it truly was.

It was a long time before she slept. The sun was streaming through the curtains when she woke again. She lay very still, cherishing the ephemeral happiness that came to her at the very edge of waking.

She wasn't alone. There was warmth behind her on the bed, a familiar weight at her back that pulled down the mattress. The pressure of another body, masculine and solid.

Peter. She kept her eyes closed. It wasn't often that Peter slept the night through and was still beside her when she woke. And when he was . . .

His hand brushed her hip, hot through the knit fabric of her long underwear. When Peter was with her in the morning, it was because he wanted to make love. She gasped silently as his palm moved down to the upper edge of her thigh and then back up again, drawing the hem of her top up and up until he found skin.

Alex shuddered. It had been so long. Her belly tightened in anticipation. Peter wanted her. He *wanted* her. His fingers stroked along her ribs with delicate tenderness. They brushed the lower edge of her breast. Her nipples hardened almost painfully.

The arousal was a release, running hot in her blood. In a moment she would roll over and into his arms. In a moment she'd give herself up to the sex, to the searing intensity of physical closeness, seizing it for as long as it lasted.

But for now Peter was caressing her gently, without his usual impatience—taking time to make her ready, to feed her excitement—and she savored it. She wouldn't ruin the moment with words. Peter wasn't usually so silent. He liked talking before and after making love. About his plans, his ambitions. Their future.

All she could hear of him now was his breathing, sonorous and steady. His palm rested at the curve of her waist, the fingers making small circles on her skin.

His fingers. Callused fingers. She could feel their slight roughness. Blunt at the tips, not tapered. Big hands.

Big hands. Too big.

Wrongness washed through her in a wave of adrenaline. She snapped open her eyes and stared at the cracked face of the old-fashioned alarm clock beside the bed. Granddad's alarm clock. And beyond, the wood plank walls of the cabin.

Not the apartment. Her cabin. Not the king-size bed but her slightly sprung double.

The hand at her waist stilled.

Alex jerked her legs and found them trapped under an implacable weight. A guttural, groaning sigh sounded in her ear.

Very slowly she turned her head.

A man lay beside her, sprawled across the bed with one leg pinning the blankets over hers. A perfectly naked, magnificently muscled stranger. His body was curled toward her, head resting on one arm. His other hand was on her skin. Straight, thick black hair shadowed his face.

Alex did no more than tense her body, but that was enough. The man moved; the muscles of his torso and flat belly rippled as he stretched and lifted his head. Yellow eyes met her gaze through the veil of his hair.

Yellow eyes. Clear as sunlight, fathomless as ancient amber. Eyes that almost stopped her heart.

For an instant—one wayward, crazy instant—Alex *knew* him. And then that bizarre sensation passed to be replaced with far more pragmatic instincts. She twisted and bucked to free her legs and shoved him violently, knocking his hand from her body. His eyes widened as he rocked backward on the narrow bed, clawed at the sheets and rolled over the far edge.

Alex tore the covers away and leaped from the bed, remembering belatedly that she'd left the dart gun outside, and Granddad's old rifle was firmly locked away in the hall closet. She spun for the door just as the man scrambled to his feet, tossing the hair from his eyes. Her hand had barely touched the doorknob when he lunged across the bed and grabbed her wrist in an iron grip.

Treacherous terror surged in her. She lashed out, and he caught her other hand. She stared at the man with his strange, piercing eyes and remembered she was not truly alone.

A wolf slept just beyond her door. A wolf that had trusted and accepted her as if she were a member of his pack. One of his own kind. A wolf that seemed to recognize the name she had given him.

"Shadow," she cried. It came out as a whisper. "Shadow!"

The man twitched. The muscles of his strong jaw stood out in sharp relief beneath tanned skin, and his fingers loosened around her wrists for one vital instant.

Alex didn't think. She ripped her arms free of his grasp, clasped her hands into a single fist, and struck him with all her strength.

Haunting, compelling, and richly
atmospheric, this dazzling novel of
romantic suspense marks the impressive
debut of a talented new author.

WALKING RAIN

by Susan Wade

*Eight years with a new name and a new identity had not
succeeded in wiping out the horrors of the past. It was time
for Amelia Rawlins to go home. Home to the New Mexico
ranch where she had spent her childhood summers. Home
to the place where she could feel her grandfather's spirit
and carry on the work he had loved. But someone knew
that Amelia had come back—Amelia, who should have
died on that long-ago day . . . who should have known
better than to think she could come back and start over
with nothing more than a potter's wheel, a handful of
wildflower seeds, and a stubborn streak. And someone was
out to see that Amelia paid in full for her crimes. . . .*

She drove up U.S. 54 from Interstate 10 because that
was the way she had always come to the ranch. Her
old pickup had held up well on the long drive from
the East Coast, but now it rattled and jounced along
the battered road. Amelia checked the rearview mirror often, making certain her potter's wheel was still
securely lashed to the bed of the truck. It was her
habit to watch her back.

    She'd reached El Paso late in the afternoon and

stopped there to put gas in the truck. Between that stop and all the Juarez traffic, it was getting on toward evening by the time she left the city and, with it, the interstate. Now the mountains of the Tularosa basin rose on either side of the two-lane road: the soaring ridge of the Guadalupes to her east and the Organ Mountains, drier, more distant, to her west. The eastern range was heavily snowed, peaks gleaming pink in the fading light, and the evening sky was winter-brilliant. Narrow bands of clouds glowed like flamingo feathers above the Organs.

She had forgotten the crystalline stillness of the air here, forgotten the sunny chill of a New Mexico winter. How had that happened? Maybe that was the price she'd paid for forgetting the things she had to forget. Part of the price.

The sun flamed on the horizon, looking as if it would flow down the mountains to melt the world, and then it sank. Its light faded quickly from the sky; already the stars were taking their turn at ruling the deep blue reaches. Amelia rolled down her window, even though the temperature outside was plunging toward freezing. The desert smelled pungent and strong, and there was a hint of pine and piñon on the wind.

It was the wind that whipped tears to her eyes. Certainly the wind; she was not a woman who wept. But she was suddenly swept by a brilliant ache of homesickness—here, now, when she was very near the only home left to her—it caught at her violently. So violently that she almost turned the truck around and went away again.

To need something so much frightened her.

But she was tired, and she had only decided to come here when she could no longer face starting over somewhere new. She'd been rootless for too long.

So the truck spun on, winding north in the star-studded darkness, past the ghostly dunes of White Sands, north and then eventually east, to a narrower road, one that ran deep into the wrinkled land at the foot of the Guadalupes.

She made her way to the Crossroads by feel, and turned left without thinking. It was unsettling to be in a place so instantly familiar. The stars had come full out; the desert was bright beneath them. An ancient seabed, the Tularosa basin was now four thousand feet above sea level, and the air was thin, rarefied, so the starlight streamed through it undiminished. Amelia could see the beacon of the observatory to the south, high on the mountain, gleaming like a fallen star itself.

And then she was there, bumping the truck off the road next to the dirt lane that led to the house. The gate was closed. A new gate, one of those metal-barred affairs. Amelia left the truck idling when she got out, not sure it would start again if she turned it off after such a long run. But when she tried to open the gate, she found it padlocked. Her grandfather never did that.

She climbed up on the gate and looked toward the ranch house, sprawling among the cottonwood trees beyond the fields. No lights. No smoke from the chimney pipe. The windows were dark vacant blanks against the pale adobe walls of the house. She could see the looming windmill, its blades turning slowly in silhouette, but nothing else moved.

So maybe the ranch hadn't been leased to some-one else. Maybe her uncle hadn't decided she was dead and sold the place off. Maybe none of the things she'd been afraid of had happened.

She should have been relieved. But the homesickness was back, wilder than ever, and she realized that some part of her had expected her grandfather to be there waiting for her.

He was dead. Bound to be. He'd been seventy-six the last time she and her kid brother had come for the summer, and that was more than a dozen years ago. But one thing she had no doubt about—that Gramps had kept his word and left the property to her. She knew he had, as surely as she knew the pattern the cottonwoods' shadow would paint on the house in summer. This place was part of her.

She went back and cut off the truck. The silence was a living one, even in February. The rustle of a mouse in its nest and the faraway cry of a hunting night bird gathered on the wind. Amelia shivered. She put on her down vest, then took her backpack and her cooler out of the truck. Nobody would bother her things, not out here. Gramps used to say they could go a week without seeing another soul on this road.

He'd been exaggerating, of course. Something he was prone to. Amelia dropped the cooler over the fence, then swung herself over the gate. She picked up the cooler and started down the lane toward the house. The smell of the desert seemed even more sharply familiar now, thick with memories. She remembered racing Michael down this road on bikes—Gramps taking the two of them to collect native grasses by the old railroad tracks, Gramma baking biscuits in the cool of the morning. So many memories. A cascade of them.

They were falling around her like rain. Amelia bowed her head and walked up the road into it.

On sale in August:

AMANDA
by Kay Hooper

THE MARSHAL AND THE HEIRESS
by Patricia Potter

TEXAS LOVER
by Adrienne deWolfe

To enter the sweepstakes outlined below, you must respond by the date specified and
follow all entry instructions published elsewhere in this offer.

DREAM COME TRUE SWEEPSTAKES

Sweepstakes begins 9/1/94, ends 1/15/96. To qualify for the Early Bird Prize, entry must be received by the date specified elsewhere in this offer. Winners will be selected in random drawings on 2/29/96 by an independent judging organization whose decisions are final. Early Bird winner will be selected in a separate drawing from among all qualifying entries.

Odds of winning determined by total number of entries received. Distribution not to exceed 300 million.

Estimated maximum retail value of prizes: Grand (1) $25,000 (cash alternative $20,000); First (1) $2,000; Second (1) $750; Third (50) $75; Fourth (1,000) $50; Early Bird (1) $5,000. Total prize value: $86,500.

Automobile and travel trailer must be picked up at a local dealer; all other merchandise prizes will be shipped to winners. Awarding of any prize to a minor will require written permission of parent/guardian. If a trip prize is won by a minor, s/he must be accompanied by parent/legal guardian. Trip prizes subject to availability and must be completed within 12 months of date awarded. Blackout dates may apply. Early Bird trip is on a space available basis and does not include port charges, gratuities, optional shore excursions and onboard personal purchases. Prizes are not transferable or redeemable for cash except as specified. No substitution for prizes except as necessary due to unavailability. Travel trailer and/or automobile license and registration fees are winners' responsibility as are any other incidental expenses not specified herein.

Early Bird Prize may not be offered in some presentations of this sweepstakes. Grand through third prize winners will have the option of selecting any prize offered at level won. All prizes will be awarded. Drawing will be held at 204 Center Square Road, Bridgeport, NJ 08014. Winners need not be present. For winners list (available in June, 1996), send a self-addressed, stamped envelope by 1/15/96 to: Dream Come True Winners, P.O. Box 572, Gibbstown, NJ 08027.

THE FOLLOWING APPLIES TO THE SWEEPSTAKES ABOVE:

No purchase necessary. No photocopied or mechanically reproduced entries will be accepted. Not responsible for lost, late, misdirected, damaged, incomplete, illegible, or postage-die mail. Entries become the property of sponsors and will not be returned.

Winner(s) will be notified by mail. Winner(s) may be required to sign and return an affidavit of eligibility/release within 14 days of date on notification or an alternate may be selected. Except where prohibited by law, entry constitutes permission to use of winners' names, hometowns, and likenesses for publicity without additional compensation. Void where prohibited or restricted. All federal, state, provincial, and local laws and regulations apply.

All prize values are in U.S. currency. Presentation of prizes may vary; values at a given prize level will be approximately the same. All taxes are winners' responsibility.

Canadian residents, in order to win, must first correctly answer a time-limited skill testing question administered by mail. Any litigation regarding the conduct and awarding of a prize in this publicity contest by a resident of the province of Quebec may be submitted to the Regie des loteries et courses du Quebec.

Sweepstakes is open to legal residents of the U.S., Canada, and Europe (in those areas where made available) who have received this offer.

Sweepstakes is sponsored by Ventura Associates, 1211 Avenue of the Americas, New York, NY 10036 and presented by independent businesses. Employees of these, their advertising agencies and promotional companies involved in this promotion, and their immediate families, agents, successors, and assignees shall be ineligible to participate in the promotion and shall not be eligible for any prizes covered herein.   SWP 3/95